DYING TO REMEMBER

DYING TO REMEMBER

A SMITHWELL FAIRIES MYSTERY

KARIN KAUFMAN

CHAPTER 1

It had rained earlier in the day, and now, as my trowel met earth in the gray afternoon, a fine drizzle began to fall. Kneeling in my front yard, head down and rain dripping from the brim of my sun hat, I dug a hole twice the size of the small rhododendron at my side, squeezed the plant from its plastic pot, and set it in the hole.

Next spring, you'll be beautiful. I sat back on my heels and admired what was left of the plant's narrow, glossy leaves. There were no purple flowers and the plant had lost most of its summer leaves, but then, it was the middle of October. In time it would bloom. And I had oodles of time.

"It'll be at least two years before that itty-bitty thing flowers."

"Out for a walk in the rain, Ray?" Still resting on my heels, I twisted back and looked up at Ray Landry, a neighbor from down the street. My friend wore a tan raincoat and shielded himself from the drizzle with a shockingly red umbrella.

"You know me, Kate. But no, I got my walk in earlier. I just wanted to bring you something." He sat himself down on a mossy landscape boulder. "But you finish what you're doing first."

"Want some tea?" Using my bare hands, I began to pull the soil back into the hole, gently pressing it around the plant.

"Maybe tomorrow. That's one big worm on top of the dirt there."

"I see." The poor thing. I set the plump earthworm I had inadvertently expelled from its home near the rhododendron's stem and sprinkled it with soil, being careful not to compact the earth about it. The rain would keep the creature moist until it could dig its way down again.

I pushed to my feet, grateful that I was still strong and agile enough to get down, dig holes, and get back up again, all with relatively little fuss. Gardening had always been a pleasure, but now it was a refuge, even in the gray days of autumn.

"Of course, the question must be asked," Ray said. "Why are you gardening in the rain?"

I glanced down at the wet knees of my jeans and then examined my boots. They were remarkably free of mud, but I scrubbed the soles on the grass anyway. *How to answer?* It was a more complicated question than Ray knew. "It's my birthday."

"I know it's your birthday. The question must still be asked."

With a sigh, I picked up my trowel and sat on another landscape boulder. My husband had set eight of them in our large front yard, and over the years they had proved useful. "It's my *fiftieth* birthday."

"I'm eighty-one, dear Kate, and I wouldn't garden in the rain." His mouth twisted in a crooked grin.

"I promised myself I'd plant that little rhododendron

6

today, come rain or high water, and I wasn't about to back out." But there was so much more to it than that. I was fifty years old. I had crossed a border, entered a new frontier from which I could never return, and I'd done it alone. "I just wish . . ."

"You wish what?" Ray rested the handle of his umbrella against his shoulder.

"Don't you wish things weren't so ordinary?"

He chuckled softly. "*You're* not ordinary."

I begged to differ. "My name is Kate Brewer, I'm a very average five foot seven inches, and I have brown hair—going gray—and brown eyes. I'm as ordinary as can be. Ten thousand women in Maine fit my description." I gestured with the trowel toward the road below us and the woods beyond. "Trudging along, day after day, year after year, getting up, going to bed, waiting and waiting."

"What's wrong with that road?"

"We live in Smithwell. Not even Smithwell Cove or Smithwell Harbor—something with a little pizazz. Just Smithwell. *Smith*. And we live on Birch Street." I aimed the trowel back at my house. "I'm at 2000 Birch Street. Not 2001 or 2023."

Ray let out a warm, full-throated laugh. "You love it here. I know you do. And I still don't understand why you're gardening in the rain and what it has to do with your birthday."

"I'm sorry. I'm just being persnickety." I had to laugh too. Truthfully, I did love my house, though it felt too big now. Like Ray's house, it sat on the hilly side of Birch Street. My large front yard sloped ever so gradually toward the road and ended, along with other yards on the block, in a flat terrace hemmed in by stone. Beyond the terrace, the ground slanted more sharply toward the meandering road. And behind our houses were even more woods, thick with balsam firs and maples. The result was an idyllic sense of isolation.

My friend's expression became solemn. "You'll get past this day. It's just another day in a long line of days, you know."

"That's the point, Ray. It makes you wonder. I always thought there was more, even when I was a kid."

"More what?"

I shrugged, at a loss to explain the longing within me. I'd felt it my entire life, and it had only grown stronger over the years. "More than what I can see, I guess."

A flicker of recognition crossed Ray's face. Somehow he understood. "Kate, there's far more to life than what you can see. Don't you know that?"

I jammed my trowel in the soil. "To be honest, no. I only know what I *see*. I know what's in front of my eyes, and I've never known anything else."

"That's not true." Ray put a hand to his chest. "You *feel* what you can't see. I know you do. And not everyone does. Some people go their whole lives without wondering what's beyond their vision. You *wonder* about it."

Sitting in the drizzle, still getting wet on my birthday, I gazed toward the woods on the far side of Birch Street. "Michael and I used to collect wild blueberries there every August," I said softly.

"Ah, the fairy woods."

"I've never imagined fairies in those woods. Not

8

like you, Ray. How do you manage without Donna? Does it get easier?"

He shook his head. "It gets harder."

"That's good to know."

"I would never lie to you. I miss her more now than four years ago, when I lost her. As time goes on, the missing gets harder. But somehow the living gets easier. You'll understand. She's waiting for me, and every day I get a little closer to seeing her again."

"I hope that day is a long way off."

"In the meantime, I have a lot to do." He unzipped his raincoat a few inches and showed me a bundle of paper held together with a large black binder clip. "That's partly why I'm here. I wasn't only being nosy about your gardening habits. I promised you my memoirs, and here's the final draft, safe from the rain."

"Good! I've been looking forward to reading that."

"You're being kind."

"And I would never lie to *you*, Ray. I can't wait to get started. Are you sure you don't want to come inside and have some tea?"

"Maybe tomorrow."

"Your memoirs should be better than the thrillers I read. You've led quite the life."

It was as though I'd flipped a switch with those few words. Ray energetically pulled the bundle from his raincoat and thrust it toward me. "I had the oddest conversation yesterday with an old friend. No, *acquaintance* better describes him. We haven't been friendly for years. Not that we dislike each other, but we run in different circles now."

I shielded his memoirs from the rain by stuffing the

9

bundle in my own raincoat. "What was odd about the conversation?"

"Our recollections of an old matter differed considerably."

I saw now that Ray's brow was lined with worry. On his walk to my house, he had carried with him whatever was weighing him down—and *something* was— but I had prattled on, not allowing him to get a word in. "That can happen, even with memories of recent events, let alone older ones."

"He hadn't forgotten. He knew I was telling the truth, but he insisted I was wrong. I wouldn't have brought the subject up, but I overheard him—in the Hannaford of all places. Why would he be talking about something that happened six years ago?"

"Who was he talking to?"

"Our illustrious town manager, Conner Welch. I was in the canned soup aisle—you know how I like my Campbell's—and this acquaintance didn't know I was there. I only meant to say hello, but he jumped and stared at me liked I'd purposely crept up on him."

"That's a funny thing to do. What was this old matter?"

"The Alana Williams case. You remember that."

"Of course I do. Everyone in Smithwell remembers."

"As long as I live, I'll never forget finding her body. Such a tragedy. She was a young woman just starting out in life, teaching at her first school. It's always disturbed me that her killer was never brought to justice."

"Her parents left the state, didn't they?"

"There were too many memories for them. Every

10

corner they turned, there she was." Ray chewed on his lower lip, and I could tell his conversation in Hannaford's had left him puzzled in any number of ways. "People don't talk about Alana Williams in the supermarket, even with the detective who ran the case. Not six years later."

"But it's almost the anniversary of her death."

"No, it doesn't come up like the weather or current news. Alana was on *my* mind, but only because I'd recently written about her for my memoirs."

"Who was this acquaintance of yours?" I asked.

"A Smithwell police detective. The one who ran the Williams case. Martin Rancourt." Ray grunted and stopped chewing his lip. "I must have misunderstood him. That could well be it. He wasn't upset, he was . . . oh, I don't know. You know what my hearing is like. I should get a hearing aid. Donna used to tell me to, but I can't be bothered. Do you realize we're sitting in the rain like a pair of nitwits?"

His change of tack was disconcerting, but I went along with it. I'd learned in the twenty years I'd known him that there was no use pressing him to talk when he wasn't ready.

"Well, then." Holding his umbrella in one hand, he used the other hand to push to his feet and then took a moment to work the muscles in his legs. "Stop by for coffee tomorrow morning? Say, about eight?"

"I'd love to."

"I'm sorry I don't have tea."

"I can drink coffee. I'm not a barbarian."

"You're too trusting, Kate."

I let go with a laugh and said, "What brought that on?"

11

"Friends are fine, but don't trust people you don't really know. Even if they say you're supposed to trust them."

"Who are you talking about?"

"No one in particular."

I bent to retrieve my trowel and stepped closer to him. "Are you all right, Ray? You seem worried. Is it that conversation or something else?"

"We'll talk tomorrow, don't you worry. We're both thriller readers, aren't we? We can put our heads together and come up with something. Imagine a town manager and a detective talking about an old murder in the soup aisle. What's that about? In the meantime, I need to do some thinking about the past. You know us old men. We do our best living in the land of the past."

"Stop that right now." I looked directly into his brown eyes and spoke in my I-ain't-playing voice. "You tell me not to live in the past, and you're right. So you stop it right now, Ray Landry. You have a lot of living to do." I thumped my raincoat where it guarded his memoirs. "More than what's here in your memoirs."

He reached out and gave me a hug—surprising because he was not a physically demonstrative man—and then started toward home.

"Take care, Ray," I called.

He halted and looked back at me. "And Kate dear, most of the time you have to *believe* to see. Everyone gets that dead backwards, you know. They say seeing is believing, but I can't tell you how wrong that is. It works the other way around. Interesting, isn't it?"

CHAPTER 2

Ray had me worried. He had always put up a good show of being lighthearted. I say "show" because he'd lost his precious wife, Donna, four years earlier, and he was *not* light of heart. So when he appeared to be concerned, he was indeed concerned. And now, of all things, he'd been reminded of the Alana Williams murder. He had happened upon the young teacher's body in the woods, a few hours after she'd been killed, and I knew from talking to Donna that it had taken weeks for him to stop seeing her whenever he shut his eyes at night.

But he'd invited me for coffee in the morning. We could talk about his memoirs, I thought, and take his mind off his troubles for a little while. In the meantime, I needed to get my nitwit self out of the rain. I turned toward my house, concentrating my attention on the empty terracotta pots by the teak bench at the front door. I knew better than to allow gloomy thoughts a foothold. It was rapidly getting dark, and the dark served to double my gloom if I didn't keep my mind occupied.

What to do with those pots? Store them in the garage? Use them for transplanted herbs? That was it. The nights were cold now, and my chives and spearmint had only survived because they were in a protected spot in the garden.

I trudged to the door, my eyes on a short stack of two upside-down pots. The uppermost pot had a triangle-shaped hole in it just below the rim, but no matter. My husband had taught me thrift, and I was proudly carrying on his tradition. I inverted a third and larger empty pot over the other two, and then, laying my trowel atop the stack, I carried the pots into the foyer and set them on the tile floor before slipping out of my gardening boots and into my clogs.

In the kitchen, I put the pots and trowel on the table, slipped out of my raincoat, and laid Ray's memoirs next to the pots. Then I rinsed my hands in the sink—taking special care to clean my wedding band—and busied myself making a pot of tea. Almond oolong, I decided. And absolutely no teabags. Making tea the proper way took time and attention. I filled the stainless kettle with water, placed it on the stove, and turned on the burner.

"What to do with the pots?" I said aloud. "The pots, the pots." Transplant the spearmint first? It was more susceptible to the cold than the chives.

I heard the trowel clatter to the table and spun back, jolted by the sudden noise.

Calm down. I'd set the trowel on top of the wet pots and it had shifted, that's all. *Take a deep breath. Count your blessings.* A woman at Michael's hospice had told me not to be surprised if my grief felt like fear. If I flinched at everyday sounds. Not to worry if I was on edge for the first six months or so. It would take time for my nerves to settle. Ten months had passed since my husband's death, and though the constant, gnawing anxiety I'd felt early on had eased and I was able to sleep at night, I still jumped like a nervous cat at unexpected noises.

"Tea, tea, make some tea," I said. That was another thing. Lately I'd been talking to myself all the time. I mean *all* the time. But I had to talk to someone, didn't I? I chose a Wedgwood teacup from my hutch, taking it and a saucer to the counter. As I drew a tin from my well-stocked tea cabinet, the doorbell rang.

I flicked off the stove and strode for the foyer. Through the glass panel on one side of the door I saw my next-door neighbor, Emily MacKenzie, holding a pizza box with a somewhat rain-splattered cake atop it. "Happy birthday!" she cried as I opened the door.

"You didn't have to do that."

"Don't be ridiculous. Of course I did."

"Come in out of the rain." I tugged on her sleeve and pulled her inside. "Is it dark chocolate? It looks like dark chocolate."

"Would I give you anything but dark chocolate on your fiftieth? It would be sacrilege, and you've suffered enough. I mean, turning fifty and all."

"Don't make fun. In two short years, you'll be in your fifties too."

"Bite your tongue." She kicked off her shoes and headed straight for my living room. "It's not just your birthday, by the way, it's our goofy TV movie night. Laurence left for Afghanistan this morning."

"What?"

"I'm exaggerating. He's off to Hungary. He won't be back for a week, and the kids aren't even in town. Whatcha say?"

"I'll get the plates. Give me your jacket and I'll put

it in the kitchen."

"You need a mudroom where your foyer is. And one of those big, open closets with lots of hooks in them."

"Got ten thousand dollars?" I called back to her.

A few minutes later we were on my couch, eating pizza and watching the sappiest movie I'd seen in a long time. Half an hour into it, I switched off the TV and asked Emily if we could talk about Ray and the six-year-old murder of Alana Williams. She shared my love of thrillers and murder mysteries, so she didn't need convincing.

"I remember that," she said, pushing a strand of her short, copper-colored hair behind one ear. "The police were useless. A load of Barney Fifes. They never arrested anyone and never even had a serious suspect. Her killer could be running around Smithwell right now, free as a bird. Probably is. Is Ray having nightmares about her body?"

"No, he had a strange conversation in the supermarket yesterday." I recounted my talk with Ray, making sure Emily understood how troubled he had been by his encounter in Hannaford's. "I haven't heard him talk about Alana Williams in almost six years," I said. "He stopped talking about her soon after he found her body. I know it's haunted him, finding her like that, but he'd put it behind him."

"Until this conversation, you mean."

"I'm having coffee with him tomorrow morning, so I'll see if he remembers anything more about the conversation."

"It's kinda weird," Emily said, working her mouth around a substantial bite of pizza. "I mean . . ." She held up a finger as she finished chewing. "Why would the town manager and the lead detective on the case be talking about Alana Williams after all this time? And in the canned soup aisle?"

"That's what Ray wondered."

"It could be a coincidence. Alana was killed in October, and maybe one of the two happened to see or hear something that sparked a memory, then met the other one and raised the subject."

"Then why was Detective Rancourt jumpy when he saw Ray? And why did he lie? Ray was positive he was lying."

"What exactly was he lying about?"

"Ray didn't say, but it was something about the case."

"It's a crazy thing to lie about. Everyone in town knows about that murder."

"I'm sure the police know much more than they ever told the public."

"So the detective remembers things differently—so what? It's been years." About to reach for another slice of pizza, Emily stopped, her hand hovering over the box. "I hear sirens." She decided against the pizza, brushing the crumbs from her hand and declaring she was ready for cake. "The cops are probably after some unsuspecting driver going five miles over the speed limit on his way home from work. Either that or someone with out-of-state plates. I guess they need more money in the town's coffers. Where's the cake knife?"

"Next to the pizza box," I said, handing her two small plates from the coffee table. As she cut the cake, my thoughts ping-ponged from Ray to chocolate and back again. "I'll take a piece to Ray tomorrow. He's got a thing for chocolate too."

"Smart man."

"Did you bake this?"

"Do I look like Martha Stewart? It's from Donahue's. They call it Bittersweet Decadence. The name alone sold me. I was torn between this and a German chocolate cake called 'German Chocolate Cake.' Needless to say, I chose 'Decadence.' Here you go."

"You made an excellent choice." Plate and fork in hand, I flopped back in my seat. "What if Conner Welch had something to do with Alana's murder? It's possible, isn't it? Or maybe Detective Rancourt was involved somehow. Maybe they were discussing how one of them got away with it and Ray overheard them, but he's not sure he heard them right."

"This is really bothering you."

"It was really bothering *Ray*. You know how even-keeled he is, or at least how even-keeled he tries to look."

Emily nodded. "Cool and calm as a cucumber. A man of the world."

"An all-around sensible man, not given to worry. But he was worried over this." The more I considered what Ray had told me, the odder it seemed. I didn't believe in coincidences. Those two men, a town manager and a detective, might have accidentally run into each other in the soup aisle, but they wouldn't have accidentally stumbled onto the subject of Alana. And Rancourt's reaction to Ray's memory of the case wasn't normal. But what had Ray's recollection of the case been and how had it differed from that of Rancourt? "We should go to the library tomorrow afternoon and look up some old articles from the *Smithwell News*. Better yet, we can access them on the internet."

"We're talking six-year-old papers."

"The library scans them. You have to pay a fee, but it's no big deal." I dug my fork into my cake. "I needed chocolate today. Thanks, Emily."

"Happy birthday to you."

I had just eaten my first bite of delicious decadence when the doorbell rang.

"Don't suppose you want to get that?" I said, reluctantly abandoning my plate and heading for the door. Through the glass panel, in the bright light at my front door, I saw a Smithwell police officer. Freckle-faced and far too young to inspire confidence. The shoulders of his uniform were soaking wet, though his cap looked snug and dry under a clear plastic rain cover. In my twenty years in Smithwell, never once had a police officer shown up at my door. In fact, except for the rare occasions when I spotted a patrol car on the road, I never saw them at all. This officer's appearance did not bode well. With mounting trepidation, I opened the door.

"Ma'am," he said with a nod. "I'm Officer David Bouchard, Smithwell Police." He glanced at the little notebook in his hand. "Is it Mrs. Brewer?"

"What is it? What's wrong?" My heart began to race.

"I'd like to talk to you about your neighbor, Ray Landry."

I stood back from the door to let him inside. "What about Ray?"

He stepped into the foyer, glancing hesitantly at his shoes. "I'll stay here. Don't want to ruin your floors."

"What is it? What about Ray?"

"I'm sorry to inform you that we found him dead inside his home, about fifteen minutes ago."

CHAPTER 3

I couldn't believe my ears. "Ray is dead?" Surely the officer meant someone else. "Ray Landry, four houses down?"

"Yes, ma'am. We're talking to his neighbors as a matter of course. When was the last time you spoke to him?"

"Hold on a minute." Bouchard was moving too fast. How could Ray be dead? "Where are the police cars?" I craned my neck for a better look at the road. "I don't see any."

"We're parked in front of his house. It's hard to see from here."

"Ray lives alone. Did he call you? Did something happen?"

"When was the last time you talked to him?" Bouchard asked.

At the sound of footsteps behind me, I turned to see Emily coming to a stop where the foyer met the living room. Judging by the expression on her face, she'd heard what Bouchard had said and was having as much trouble as I was taking it in.

"Um . . ." Needing to sit, I pulled the door shut, walked past Emily, and sank to the arm of my couch. *Not*

Ray. Please not Ray. Let him be wrong. When I invited the officer to join me in the living room, he declined, pointing at his muddy shoes.

"I'm fine here, ma'am. I can hear you standing right here."

"I saw him about two hours ago," I said. "I was in my front yard, planting a rhododendron, and he was taking a walk."

"Are you sure you're talking about the Ray Landry on Birch?" Emily said. She spun back to me, disbelief in her eyes, then joined me in the living room, perching herself on the edge of the coffee table.

"I don't understand," I said. "What happened to him, and why did you go to his house?"

"He called 911," Bouchard said. "It was a hang-up call, but we investigate those."

Emily swallowed hard. "How did he die?"

"You are?"

"Emily MacKenzie from next door. To your left as you go outside. My husband is out of town, so there's no one there."

"Right now I can't tell you how he died," the officer said. "Tomorrow or the next day the coroner's office will—"

"Now hold on," I said, bounding from the couch. "He's my neighbor, and if someone killed him, we need to—"

"Killed him?" Bouchard was incredulous. "This is just a routine call on his neighbors. Did he complain of chest pain, did he complain of food poisoning—that kind of thing. It looks like he had a heart attack—and you did *not* hear that from me."

"That's not possible," I said.

"He was eighty-two, wasn't he?"

"Eighty-one," I replied, wondering what Ray's age had to do with it. But to be fair, the officer didn't know what I knew: Ray was healthy as a horse. A strong heart, a sharp mind.

"So either way, he wasn't young." Bouchard nodded sagely. No doubt he'd been taught that question-quelling nod at the police academy.

"He was healthy," I said. "He worked in his garden all the time."

"Are you saying he wasn't attacked?" Emily asked.

"There was no sign of an attack or struggle or anything of that nature," Bouchard said. "It looks like he died peacefully, eating soup. And I did *not* tell you that."

"Eating soup?" I said.

"At his kitchen table, yep," the officer replied. "It's possible he had a heart attack—and that's all I can tell you."

"Wait a minute," I said. "You said he called 911 but hung up?"

"It happens all the time."

"Not to people I know it doesn't."

"He was eighty-one, Mrs. Brewer." He raised his cap and gave his short brown hair a ruffle. "That's about it. I'm sorry, and thank you for your time."

"Wait a second. Is that all you're going to ask me? Is that all you're asking other people?"

"If you can think of anything else, let me know." He dug into his uniform and produced a card. "Here's my number. Feel free to call, or call the station."

I was on the verge of telling Bouchard about the

23

conversation Ray had heard in the supermarket when I thought better of it. One of the last things my friend had said to me was that I was too trusting. And he'd especially cautioned me not to trust anyone I didn't really know. Well, I didn't know Bouchard from Adam. "Officer Bouchard, I just told you Ray was healthy."

He gave me a saccharine smile. I was about to be told how foolish I was. "The coroner can make that determination. One thing I will tell you—and you didn't hear *this* from me either—is that he was eating mushroom soup, and it looks like the mushrooms weren't from Hannaford's, if you catch my drift. You get it, right? Bad mushrooms and a man of his age are not compatible."

I glared at him. "Ray foraged for mushrooms all the time, along with a lot of other things. Maine is carpeted with edible wild mushrooms, and he was an expert at them. He taught me and my husband to forage in the woods across the street."

Bouchard's eyes narrowed, and for a brief moment I thought I'd gotten through to him.

I hadn't. In the officer's judgment, Ray was old, his ticker had ticked its last, and that was that.

"Well, Mrs. Brewer, my guess is his heart gave out and he just happened to be eating soup at that moment. I've seen heart attacks before, and that's what it looked like to me. At his age, it's to be expected. To be blunt, we're just going door to door to let his neighbors know what happened since we had the sirens going. But let me know if you think of anything else," he said, tipping his hat as he moved for the door. "And again, my condolences."

I stopped myself—just barely—from saying

something rude before I shut the door.

Emily walked up to me, hugged me, and then stepped back. "I can't believe it. I saw Ray yesterday. It's like you said—he's healthy as a horse. How could this happen?"

"That's what I'd like to know. All that officer talked about was Ray's age and how the mushrooms weren't store-bought."

We returned to my living room and slumped into the couch, trying to take it all in. Ray was gone. That sweet man who had taught me and Michael to forage for wild blueberries and wild leeks in the woods. Who had taught me most of what I now knew about gardening. He had *not* picked bad mushrooms. Simple fact.

Emily took a shuddering breath. "We don't like coincidences, do we?"

"Ray overhears talk about Alana Williamson's murder, he's concerned enough to mention it to me, and two hours later he's dead? No, we don't like coincidences."

"I couldn't help notice you didn't tell that officer what Ray heard in the supermarket."

"I was going to, but Ray told me not to trust anyone."

Emily's eyes went wide. "Really?"

"You I can trust, of course, but he said not to trust anyone I don't know. Unfortunately, that leaves six thousand people, just about the entire population of Smithwell, not to trust." I sighed and brushed my bangs from my eyes. "And now that I've told you about what Ray heard, *you* shouldn't repeat it to anyone you don't know. As a matter of fact, don't repeat it, period."

"Kate, do you realize that the person who killed Alana six years ago may have killed Ray?"

"I wonder if his next-door neighbors saw a visitor at his house this evening."

"The way this street bends, it's hard to see your neighbors unless you're way out on your front lawn."

"True." Incapable of sitting still, I began to pace my living room, taking only five strides in each direction before I encountered furniture and had to spin about and pace the other way. "That officer wanted to brush his hands of Ray's death. Emily, I don't think they're going to investigate. What do I do? I wish you could have seen Ray. When he told me not to trust anyone, he meant it. I don't dare tell the police about our conversation. Just before he left, he said we both read thrillers so we could put our heads together and come up with something."

"An answer to Alana's murder?"

"That must be it. Because then he said he had some thinking to do about the past." I stopped and spread my hands. "If only he'd said more to me."

Emily got up from the couch and started doing a little pacing of her own. "Okay, hang on a minute. We're two jumps ahead of ourselves. If Ray died of a heart attack, an autopsy will tell us that, and if he was murdered, we'll find that out too. Right? Bouchard said the coroner would make a determination in a day or two. Until then"—she stopped dead in her tracks and swiveled to face me, her blue eyes narrowing—"we say zip. Nada." With her thumb and forefinger she made a key-locking motion across her lips.

"Agreed."

The tragedy of Ray's death was beginning to sink

in—for both of us, I think. Although we remained standing, we both stopped talking, and we stood there, limp-armed and slouching. It was as though the air had been let out of our figurative tires.

"Are you as tired as I am?" Emily asked.

"At least. I can't believe what just happened. Let's call it a night."

"Breakfast here tomorrow morning? I'll bring chocolate croissants." She gazed down at the coffee table. "I'm leaving you with a mess."

"Hardly. Anyway, cleaning up will take my mind off things for a few minutes."

"I'm sorry for your lousy birthday."

"The cake wasn't lousy. Tomorrow I'll wrap a couple pieces for you."

Emily got her jacket from the kitchen and I walked her to the door, watching her as she headed for her house. For an instant it crossed my mind that she might be in danger, but I dismissed the thought. No one knew Ray had spoken to *me* about his Hannaford encounter, let alone that I'd talked to Emily.

She made her way across my lawn and then along the flagstone path that Michael had laid between the two houses more than a decade ago. Though we were technically next-door neighbors, our homes were half an acre apart, and the path made up for the lack of sidewalks. Michael and Laurence, Emily's husband, had taken turns shoveling snow from the path in the winter. Now it was Laurence's job. When he wasn't in Hungary or Afghanistan.

I shut and locked my door, marched to my kitchen, and then checked the deadbolt on my back door. There was nothing wrong with an abundance of caution. When I turned back, I was confronted by the sight of the terracotta pots and the dirty trowel. And Ray's memoirs. His life tapped out on his old electric typewriter and held together by a binder clip. I'd momentarily forgotten about his precious bundle of papers.

Feeling too upset to go to sleep, and wanting to delve into Ray's memoirs, I decided to make a cup of herbal tea and take it and the memoirs to bed for a long read. I flicked on the stove, got the kettle going, and sat down at the table.

"All Officer Bouchard can see is your age, Ray," I said aloud. The police weren't going to look at anything else. Ray was in his eighties, so of course he'd had a heart attack. His had been a "natural" death, as if death was at all natural. My only hope was that the coroner wasn't the fool Bouchard apparently was.

Propping my elbows on the table, I let my chin sink into my hands and stared at the title page of Ray's memoirs. It read, quite simply, "My Life." A flood of love and grief for my friend welled up inside of me, and for a moment, I let the tears fall. Then I got down to work.

I flipped the page up over the binder clip and immediately noticed a handwritten note: "Kate, I've gone over this in my mind and I think my memory is quite good and potentially useful. Look at chapter 14 on Alana Williams. But I will talk to you about this."

CHAPTER 4

The kettle let loose with a piercing whistle and I jumped in my seat, nearly knocking Ray's manuscript off the table. *For pity's sake, it's only water on the boil.* I turned off the stove, fixed myself a cup of spearmint tea, and sat down again, all while trying to talk myself into getting a grip. On top of losing Michael, now I'd lost Ray, one of the sweetest, strongest, kindest men I'd ever known. He'd been an anchor in my life after Michael died, though I'd never told him that.

I took a sip of tea and, trying to calm myself, turned my attention to the terracotta pots on the table. For the first time I noticed a green film covering the bottom of the top pot and the rims of the other pots. Was it algae? Moss? I leaned a little closer. Whatever the green stuff was, it smelled. And if it was mold, the pots needed to go straight back outside. I refused to have that stink in my house.

And now that I looked, the pot I'd set on top of the stack had a big crack in it too, extending from the rim to almost the middle of the pot. A hole near the top of a pot was one thing, but a long fracture meant the pot would soon break in two. Still, I could shatter the pots to pieces and use the shards to cover holes in other pots. "That's it, then, I'm throwing these pots out," I said. Loudly, forcefully, as if declaring, out of sheer habit, my intentions to Michael. I stood and took hold of the stack.

Instantly, I heard a distinct flutter—like wings against a pot—and let go of the stack, horrified that a small creature was trapped inside one of them, fighting to get out. A sparrow? A baby sparrow?

A mouse?

"Not in here!" I cried. "I hate mice!" I grabbed the stack again, but as I lifted it, my palms slipped on the green slime.

The pots fell to the table and rolled to the floor, cracking open like giant clay eggs and releasing a creature with beating wings into the kitchen.

My hands flew to my face and I staggered backward, sending my chair toppling.

With my back pressed hard to the wall, I slowly spread my fingers, searching the kitchen. Birds in trees were lovely, but one trapped inside your house was a nightmare. Those flapping wings. Those *droppings*. Worse, a bird might die before it made it outside again.

A tiny squeak from the hutch caused me to reassess the nature of the creature. Mice didn't fly, but then again, generally speaking, birds didn't squeak like mice. So what did I have here? A baby, perhaps. A baby bird just learning to fly.

I dropped my hands. "You poor, sweet thing," I said, inching forward. "Are you a baby?"

"No."

I halted, my eyes now riveted to the hutch. I did *not* hear that, I told myself. Wild birds don't talk. Simple fact. Anyway, I couldn't see a bird among the china in my hutch, and even a baby bird would be visible there. My hyperactive nerves were once again playing tricks on my mind. *Take a deep breath.*

"I said I'm not a baby."

"No!" I screamed and flung myself back against the wall, my heart pounding in my chest, panic flooding my senses. Training my eyes on the hutch, I sidestepped to the counter, wrenched open a drawer, and pulled out the first knife I laid my hands on.

Instantly I heard another squeak—this one different from the last and so pitiable that I dropped the knife on the counter. "I won't hurt you," I whispered.

A moment later, two tiny hands rose from inside a Wedgwood cup and grasped the rim.

I sucked in my breath. Had I lost my mind? I gathered up what remained of my courage and edged toward the hutch. The hands I saw weren't much larger than split peas, but they were undeniably hands—with four fingers and a thumb the color of pale human flesh.

When I was three feet from the cup, the creature raised its head above the rim.

I gasped and froze in place. "Oh, Lord, Lord."

"I won't hurt you," the creature said, its voice high-pitched but soft as honey. As two wings unfurled behind its head, it rose slowly in the cup. "Don't be afraid."

"Oh, please no."

The creature's wings were rose-petal pink, fading to an ivory blush closer to its body, and like butterfly wings, each of its wings was in two parts, with a more angular top and a separate, rounder bottom. Its hair was short, wavy, and a shimmering light brown, and it wore . . . what? Something pink and yellow. Soft looking, like its

31

wings, and crinkled where it was gathered at the creature's waist. A top and . . . shorts?

"This is madness," I said. My courage deserting me, I stumbled back from the hutch. "I'm not seeing this. I am *not* seeing this."

"I've watched you," the creature said.

I let out a strangled laugh. "Oh, great. That's great," I said, turning away from the creature. I squeezed my eyes shut, counted to ten, and turned back. It was still there. This *thing* inside a teacup. "This is insane."

"No, it's not."

"Oh, Lord, I didn't mean what I said to Ray about not wanting things to be ordinary." Again I shut my eyes. "Give me ordinary, please. I don't want to lose my mind. I can't lose my mind. Give me ordinary."

Slowly I opened my left eye.

"I won't hurt you, Kate," the creature repeated.

It called me Kate. The hair at the back of my neck stood on end. "You know my name?"

I raced from the kitchen and made straight for the front door. I grabbed the doorknob, but my hand, still slimy from the pots, slipped, so I grabbed again—this time with both hands—and yanked open the door. In one swift movement, I strode across the threshold, shot a glance over my shoulder, and pulled the door shut behind me.

Outside, my heart still thumping, I forced myself to take deep, calming breaths. Either that *thing* in my house was real or I was losing it, and at that moment, I wasn't sure which of the two possibilities was worse.

A fine rain was falling, but I resisted the impulse to go back inside and instead took deep, cleansing breaths. It wasn't until I saw a dark SUV pass slowly along Birch, as if scrutinizing the homes on my side of the street, that I thought better of standing in the rain and possibly putting myself in harm's way. Though I was relieved when the SUV continued west on Birch, the vehicle was a reminder that Bouchard aside, there was a killer in Smithwell and I needed to act like it.

I went back inside, closed my front door, and stood silently in the foyer, listening. There were no squeaks, no flutter of wings. I moved cautiously toward the kitchen, my eyes alert. At the kitchen table, I steeled myself and turned back to face the hutch. "It can't be!"

The creature was sitting next to a teacup, its wings spread wide, its legs dangling over the shelf edge. My muscles went weak and I dropped to a chair.

"Why are you afraid? *I'm* the little one."

The creature was indeed little. About four inches high, I guessed, if you didn't include the tips of her wings. "Because you're not supposed to be here. You don't exist."

"But you're talking to me."

"That's the problem. Michael always said I let my imagination run wild sometimes, and now I've really lost my grip."

"I've watched you."

"You said that before, and believe me, it doesn't sound any better the second time around."

"Why?"

Maybe I *wasn't* losing my grip on reality. This thing was talking to me, wasn't it? Forming sentences, asking questions. Sure, I was skittish these days. I talked to myself too much and jumped at loud sounds, but I'd never

33

gone over the edge. Never even got close to it. I was, on the whole, a sensible person. "What are you?"

The creature's lips curved into a sweet smile. "It's about time you asked. I'm a fairy."

I flopped back in my chair. So Ray Landry's tales about Smithwell's fairyland woods weren't tales after all. Or were they? Had he made up stories to distract me after Michael died? "A friend of mine once told me that fairies existed, but he was joking."

"Ray of the Forest."

I stared. "Yes, Ray."

"Ray of the Forest died today."

"I know," I managed to say. "He was my friend. He was a good man."

"He treated the ladybugs and crickets with kindness. Like you do."

The fairy stood to her bare feet, her wings bending backward as she moved. They appeared to act as counterbalances, keeping her on the shelf even as she leaned over the edge.

An instant later her butterfly wings flapped forward and she took horizontally to the air, speeding in my direction.

Stunned, I threw myself back in my seat and covered my face with my hands.

"I'm on the table now," the fairy said a second later. "I won't move again."

I peeked through my fingers to make certain the creature wasn't moving and then let my hands fall. "Next time say something when you're going to do that."

"Yes, Kate."

"How do you know Ray?"

"I met him in the forest. I talked to him, and he kept me secret and safe when it was cold. I'll miss him."

"When did you meet him?"

"The last time of falling leaves. One year ago."

"You speak English well."

"Of course I do. I live here."

"How silly of me." I watched as the fairy sat down cross-legged a mere two feet from my face. For the first time I noticed her luminous green eyes, so piercing it was as though they were lit from behind. "Do you have a name?" I asked.

"Minette."

"That's very pretty. Do you have a last name?"

"I'm Minette Plummery of the Smithwell Forest."

"Okay. Sure." Pressing my palms to the table, I rose to my feet. Feeling a little wobbly, I stood in place, letting the strength return to my legs.

"You're still afraid of me."

"No, I'm afraid of myself. You're not supposed to exist, and I'm sure not supposed to be talking to you."

"There are more things in heaven and earth than you dream of, Kate."

"You're quoting Shakespeare?"

"God gave him those words."

"You know that for a fact, do you?"

"You don't believe in God?"

"Of course I do."

Minette scrunched up her face. "God created me. Just because you never saw me before doesn't mean I don't exist. There are all kinds of things *you* don't see."

I opened a cabinet under the sink and began to rummage through it. *I'm arguing with a fairy. Earlier today they didn't exist, and now I'm arguing with one.* "I have things to do, Minette. My friend died today, and I don't believe he died of a heart attack. Even if the coroner says so, I won't believe it."

"Are you getting a knife?"

"I'm getting a flashlight. I'm going to Ray's house. He gave me a key to his back door."

"You shouldn't do that."

"There it is." I set the flashlight on the counter, shut the cabinet, and looked back at Minette. "What do you know about Ray's death?"

"Only that he died, and that it's not good for neighbors to see a flashlight in Ray's house at night. They'll call the police and put you in trouble."

"Put me in trouble?" I almost smiled. "You may have a point."

"Go when it's daytime," Minette instructed. "Go tomorrow."

"Are you sure you don't know something about his death?"

"I wasn't in his house when he died. I followed him when he walked to your house, and I went into your flower pot to stay out of the rain."

"He didn't have a heart attack, did he?"

"Never, Kate."

CHAPTER 5

Though I was still too antsy to go to bed, I wondered how I was going to sleep that night, knowing that Minette was in the house. Even if I showed her the door, I thought, she could slip back in through an unpatched hole or some weak point where the house met the foundation or . . . who knew? If mice could get in, so could fairies.

But I was determined to ignore her until she went away. That was my brilliant plan. My return to sanity. She lived in the Smithwell woods, didn't she? She probably needed to go back to her home in a tree or a log, maybe nibble on a little autumn cress or whatever fairies ate. If I ignored her, if I set my thoughts on Ray's death and Alana William's unsolved murder, Minette would leave, and eventually my pulse would return to normal.

I dumped the broken pots in my kitchen trash bin and took my now-lukewarm tea and Ray's memoirs to the living room—I didn't feel safe going to bed, even with a closed and locked bedroom door—and settled into my armchair by the fireplace, right across from Michael's chair. It had been his favorite place to read and talk, especially as October nights grew colder. After re-reading Ray's note on the first page, I flipped through the pages until I found chapter 14, the one on Alana.

Much of what Ray had written wasn't news to me and didn't seem noteworthy in any way that would explain who had killed Alana. She'd been a twenty-four-year-old teacher in her first year at Smithwell Middle School when, six weeks into the school year, she was found dead in the woods, two miles from her school and about a mile from Ray's house. He had been foraging for acorns and chokeberries when he found her—just hours after she'd been killed. Alana hadn't shown up for classes after her lunch break, but no one had raised an alarm.

"I was grateful I had found her and not kids playing hooky in the woods," Ray wrote. "Her body looked peaceful, but her face did not. A knife with a short handle was still lodged in the right side of her neck. She was wearing a blue dress and a long, hooded jacket. The jacket was unbuttoned but almost closed, as if the killer had neatened it out of respect. Alana was wearing a green and brown plaid scarf, which was blown back away from her neck, and a silver-colored heart-shaped necklace. I wasn't sure on first look what had happened to her because there was almost no blood. I remember looking around me. I was suddenly fearful and sensed that the madman who had killed her might be near. But my father, as I've said, had been a policeman, so that part of my upbringing took over, and I studied the scene before leaving Alana there and calling the Smithwell Police Department from the closest house."

I heard a low rustle and raised my chin as Minette swayed like a lazy butterfly toward the couch to my left.

"I'm moving slowly and slowly," she said. "See?"

My throat suddenly dry, I nodded and said nothing.

She dropped to the top of the couch, scooted

38

forward, and then, her wings vibrating, drifted gently downward until she landed on the seat cushion. "I heard the policeman talk about Ray of the Forest," she said, sitting cross-legged. "He was my friend."

I took a quick sip of tea so my dry lips wouldn't stick to my dry gums. "I'm sorry, Minette. He was my friend too. Why do you call him Ray of the Forest?"

"That's where I met him."

"He foraged."

"I showed him where to pick berries and leeks and mushrooms."

"You did?" I shivered a little at the thought. Mushrooms?

"Kate, why are you still afraid of me?"

"You're not supposed to be here."

"But I *am* here. And because I *am*, I'm supposed to be."

It was hard to fight the logic of that. But what did I really know about this creature? She had wings, liked ladybugs, had a voice like honey, and could fly like a supersonic jet when she wanted to. That was about the extent of it. This thing, undoubtedly capable of sneaking in and out of my house, was in my living room, and I had no idea what she really was. For all I knew, she'd suggested that Ray pick the mushrooms he had for his last meal. *They're safe, Ray of the Forest. Eat them.*

I held up Ray's memoirs. "Ray wrote this."

"I watched him write it."

"I'm hoping it will help me discover a few things."

"You must help, Kate. I can ask no one else."

Minette's eyes glistened, and then she blinked and a tear slid down each cheek. It broke my heart a little. It

39

was such a human expression of grief, but then, her face was entirely human. Sweeter and with an innocent beauty, but a human face in miniature.

Maybe I was getting paranoid as well as delusional. Minette seemed genuinely sad at Ray's passing, and she hadn't tried to hurt me. Still, a creature everyone thought to be mythical—including me—was sitting on my couch, telling me I had to help her. I needed to talk to someone, but there was no one for me to turn to. Michael and Ray were gone, and Emily would think I was mad if I told her about Minette.

"I'm trying to help," I said. "If Ray was murdered, I promise I'll *try* to find who did it."

Minette wiped away her tears. "And I'll help you too."

I leaned forward, hugging the memoirs to my chest. "Can you think of anyone who might have wanted to kill him? Did someone angry come to the house? Did he have an angry conversation on the phone?"

"He was never angry. He was sad sometimes, though."

"And you never saw or heard anyone angry with him?"

"No."

"What about yesterday, when he came back from the supermarket? Did he seem different?"

A look of intense concentration came over Minette's face. Her tiny hands closed into fists, and as she brought them up under her chin, her eyes narrowed. "Yes, he was different." She tilted back her head, seemingly trying to recall Ray, and as she did, her wings lay back, flattening like a dog's ears. "He said, 'My dad was a policeman, and

40

I know what I saw. What were they doing there, Minette? I don't trust them They both looked like chased rabbits, and the guilty chased rabbits flee when no man pursues.'"

That's so Ray, I thought, leaning back, resting the memoirs on my lap. "You have a very good memory."

Minette smiled and unclenched her fists. "He was talking to me, and I always listened to him. He talked to himself, too, like you do."

"Ray committed Alana's murder scene to memory, and he was good at that sort of thing."

"He was trying to find out who killed that woman."

"He was thinking about her again, maybe for the first time in years, because he was writing his memoirs."

"That's why someone killed him."

"I don't know that for sure, but I'm going to check out his house and see what I can find."

As she leaned forward, her wings flapped backward, nearly touching behind her. "You must be very careful, Kate. You must promise me."

My fear of Minette—and of myself for seeing her—began to melt a little. "I promise."

"I will go with you to his house."

"No, I'll take Emily. You stay here." *Stay here?* I was surprised as Minette was to hear those words come out of my mouth. But obviously I couldn't stuff her in my pocket and risk Emily seeing her, and I needed a human-sized lookout to watch for anyone coming to Ray's door while I snooped around. Ray had given me a key to his back door, so at least I couldn't be accused of breaking and entering, but I doubted the police would look favorably on my digging around a crime scene—*if* they would deign to call it that.

41

"I will stay here."

"I'll go first thing in the morning. Hopefully before anyone else shows up at his house. His son lives in California, and I'm sure he'll need to settle Ray's affairs. In the meantime, I need to keep reading his memoirs."

"Then I must have sleep time," Minette said. "If . . ."

She hesitated, as if expecting a response, and I realized she was asking to sleep in my house, though I knew full well she could do what she pleased and I was powerless to stop her. Shooing a fairy out of a house was tantamount to evicting a fly. It wasn't practical.

"Sleep on the couch," I said. "Or wherever you want to."

Her little face broke into a grin. "The pretty teacup."

"Oh, well, sure. Whatever you—"

But she had already taken off, breaking the sound barrier, I was sure, as she flew for my kitchen.

So Ray had known about this creature for a year and had remained silent. As I sat there, thumbing the pages of his life story, I wondered if it was because I'd chuckled when he'd talked about fairies. Had he been testing me, judging if it was safe to tell me about his discovery? But how could I have known that he was serious?

"Well," I said aloud, getting back to his memoirs. "I'm listening now, Ray. Tell me what you know."

I carried on from where I'd left off, with Ray at a nearby house calling the police. "I talked to the homeowner for a few minutes and then decided to go back to the scene," he wrote. "I couldn't leave Alana alone because it didn't seem right. But the first cops were already there when I got back: Detective Martin Rancourt and Officer Marie St. Peter. Officer St. Peter was already taping off the scene, and neither of them would let me anywhere near Alana. That was understandable and proper police procedure, even though I had stood right over the poor girl ten minutes before. St. Peter asked me to wait for her by her squad car, and soon, after two more officers arrived, she took my statement in her car. I remember looking at Rancourt through the back window. He had crouched down over the body. I could tell that like me, he was recording every element of the scene with his eyes. I told St. Peter everything. Every single detail, including the odd feeling that the killer was nearby when I first arrived. After that, I was asked to leave the area."

When I flipped the page, I saw another handwritten note in the top margin: "Coffee."

"That's weird," I said. Ray wouldn't have started a grocery list on the page. His memoirs were too important to him. So what did "Coffee" mean?

As I read on, another puzzle niggled at me. How had Ray's version of events differed from Detective Rancourt's? Which of Rancourt's facts had he disputed? He hadn't underlined or circled anything on this page or the one before, so how would I find out? I flipped to the next page, and then the next and the next, but there were no more notes, no underlining—nothing. The most obvious solution was to ask Rancourt what Ray had said to him in Hannaford's, but in addition to that being a nerve-racking prospect, I wasn't sure I'd hear the truth in reply.

Returning to Ray's story, I read, "At first I thought Alana was killed elsewhere and her body was taken to the woods, but the fallen leaves were barely disturbed—only

43

as if a small struggle had taken place. There were no drag marks in the leaves and no soil on the heels of her shoes. Then I remembered my father telling me that murderers who knew the human body knew where to stab the internal carotid artery so that almost all of the bleeding is internal. I thought then that either a woman or a man could have killed Alana. It wouldn't have taken great strength."

It was astonishing. Except for the fact that Alana's body was found in the woods, all this was news to me. The police had kept mum on the case, presumably because it was still open, and virtually none of what Ray wrote had ever been reported in the newspapers. Now Ray was talking about Alana for the first time in six years, writing down his version of the story. Had he been killed to keep him quiet?

CHAPTER 6

That night I slept well, even with Minette snoozing in a
teacup in my kitchen. In fact, I dozed off while reading
Ray's memoirs and then toddled off to bed without
checking on her. My fear of her had mostly disappeared,
along with the fear that I was experiencing hallucinations.
I felt comforted in a strange way, knowing that another
living creature was nearby and for the first time in months
I wasn't alone at night. I thought having her in the house
was rather like having a pet sleeping at the foot of your
bed—though I didn't dare tell her that.

As I headed into the kitchen the next morning, I
called out a hello, but she wasn't in the hutch or anywhere
else I could see. What did fairies have for breakfast? I
wondered. I hadn't seen her eat a single thing. I had so
many questions. Silly ones, like who made her clothes,
and harder ones, like were there any more of her kind in
the woods across Birch Street.

I made tea and toast, in case Emily forgot the
croissants, moving with the sort of energy that came with
a newfound purpose in life. This would not be an ordinary
day spent puttering around my garden, much as I loved to
do that. No, I was going to find out who had killed Ray.
First I'd snoop around his house. Later, if I could work up

the nerve, I'd talk to this Detective Rancourt. And I'd find out if Marie St. Peter was still on the police force.

When the doorbell rang, I whispered loudly for Minette to hide herself, though being a fairy in a human world she had to be more than adept at that. I found Emily standing on my front step, a box of pastries in her hand and a sour expression on her face. She headed for my kitchen, telling me she'd just spoken to Officer Bouchard. I braced myself for the news and invited her inside.

"What did Bouchard say?" I asked. "Want some almond tea?"

Emily plopped down at the table and opened her box of chocolate croissants. "A quick cup, yeah. Bouchard said the coroner hadn't seen Ray yet."

"So they're not in any hurry," I said, turning on my stove and getting the kettle going again. "Yesterday Bouchard said the report would come out tomorrow or the next day. That means we need to hit Ray's house immediately. Like in five minutes. I don't want the police to walk in on us."

"What do you mean?"

I joined her at the table and grabbed myself a croissant before she could eat all four of them. And eat them she would. Emily's sweet tooth was more voracious than mine. "I need to see Ray's house for myself. I want to look at his house the way he looked at Alana's murder scene. You have to read his memoirs. He noticed everything at the scene." I proceeded to tell Emily what I'd read last night, making special note of Alana's jacket, necklace, mud-free shoes, and scarf.

"And another thing," I said. "He wrote the word 'coffee' on one of the pages."

"That's odd."

I made us tea—my second cup—and checked my watch. We needed to get going. "Let's walk through the woods to get to his house."

A minute later, stuffing croissants in our mouths, we were on the move. I found my cell phone in the living room and slid it into my jeans pocket. Then I grabbed my key ring from a hook on the back door and we headed outside. If the police were at Ray's house, I could simply say I wanted to talk to them. Anyway, the police seemed confident Ray's house wasn't a crime scene, and if it wasn't, they would have no problem with me, key in hand, checking out my friend's house, making sure it was locked tight after his death.

To avoid neighbors' prying eyes, we first marched into the woods behind my house and then cut left. Four houses down and still in the woods, we turned left again and strode to Ray's back door. Seeing no one about, I slipped the key into the latch and stepped inside.

"Hello?" I called, shutting the door. "Anyone here?"

The morning sun, filtered through the sheer white curtains on the door and the window next to it, gave the large kitchen a bright, homey quality, despite Ray's almost palpable absence. I scanned the room, my eyes darting from two open shelves neatly lined with quart-sized Ball jars to his weathered-looking kitchen table and his almost spare counters: a single pot of herbs, a canister labeled "Sugar," and a coffeemaker. On top of his stove was a saucepan one-third full of mushroom soup.

"That's the last meal he cooked," Emily said, bending low and taking a sniff of the pot. "These mushrooms look and smell fine to me, even after sitting

47

out all night. Do you think the police took samples?"

"If they intend to tell people Ray died from bad mushrooms, they'd *better* have taken samples. Don't touch anything."

I took my phone out and moved closer to the table. At one end of it was a cutting board, a knife, and a dozen or so slivers of beige-colored mushrooms, now slightly shriveled. To my eyes, they looked like grocery-bought button mushrooms after I'd scrubbed them of the browner parts of their skins. At the other end of the table, beneath a window, there was a white bowl half filled with soup. In it floated slices of mushrooms, though they were browner, darkened by cooking.

I snapped a photo and turned away, toward the Ball jars on the open shelves. Ray's magnificent collection of nuts, berries, seeds, and herbs. "Look how he's lined them up perfectly," I said. "He had his fussy side."

Each jar was labeled with black pen on a white sticker in Ray's handwriting: "Roasted Hazelnuts," "Ground & Dried Wild Leeks," "Rose Hips," "Roasted Chicory." It was a forager's grocery store, arranged not in alphabetical order but by type of food.

"Think of the hours of foraging those represent," Emily said.

Starting on my left and moving right, I carefully perused the two long rows of jars. I'd been in Ray's kitchen many times before, and to my eyes, nothing seemed amiss. Using a kitchen towel I found hanging by a loop on a cabinet, I took the jar labeled "Mushrooms" from the shelf and unscrewed the lid, trying as best I could to not erase possible fingerprints or leave my own behind. The mushrooms smelled earthy, like any dried mushrooms, but I was no expert.

There wasn't much in Ray's refrigerator. Milk, bread, eggs, orange juice, and what looked like half a homemade raisin pie. In the freezer were more of his foraging treasures, this time neatly stacked in labeled plastic bags: fiddleheads, dandelion greens, mustard greens, and more. Nothing out of the ordinary for Ray.

Next we headed into the living room. It too was bright—the police hadn't bothered to shut the drapes— and it, like the kitchen, was a clean and uncluttered space, but that was Ray to the core. Neatness and order had been paramount in his life, even as a widower in his eighties. I'd always thought he'd caught the order bug from his father, who had been in the Marines before becoming a cop, and I'd often wondered if Ray had driven Donna half mad with his tidiness.

There was a writing desk in one corner of the living room, and on it sat a chrome lamp, his black electric typewriter, and a box of typing paper. Using the sleeve of my jacket, I opened the desk drawer. I found store receipts, mostly from Hannaford's, paperclipped together, a brand-new ribbon cartridge for the typewriter, two letters from a woman named Sheila Abbottson of Central Maine Realty, and a pamphlet titled *Fairy Lore and Horticulture in Smithwell* by a woman named Irene Carrick.

If Ray, who evidently talked to fairies on the sly, thought the pamphlet was worth reading, then I too needed to give it a look. I folded it, stuck it in my back pocket, and returned to the desk drawer.

"Whatcha got there?" Emily said.

Shoot. My friend had been studying Ray's single

bookshelf, but *still* she'd seen me pocket the small booklet. "It's a pamphlet on fairy lore published by the Smithwell Garden Society. I thought I'd give it a read."

Emily laughed. "Ray and his fairies."

My head jerked at her words.

She crossed the room and laid a gentle hand on my arm. "Are you all right?"

"I'm fine. But I want to know what happened to Ray. I don't like that Bouchard was jumping to conclusions."

"Like how mushrooms killed him? We don't buy it."

I walked over to his front window and directed my gaze at the woods across Birch Street. "Ray knew what was safe to eat and what wasn't. He foraged for decades, Emily. He was incredibly knowledgeable, and he knew those woods inside and out."

"I prefer to get my food from the supermarket, but you're right. He knew his stuff."

"He loved those woods. Spring or winter, it didn't matter."

Emily began to inspect the drawer of an end table, pulling it open using the hem of her brown heathered sweater. "That's why he has that pamphlet. He used to tell me those woods were full of fairies." She chuckled softly. "He had a vivid imagination. I think he half believed he could see them. He used to quote that line from Shakespeare—the one about there being more things in heaven and earth than we can dream of."

"Yes."

"I'll miss him."

"I'd sure like to talk to him now."

50

"You two talked a lot."

"But not much about fairies."

"Because he knew you're a cynic," Emily said, again chuckling. "On the other hand, he knew I had a soft spot. Or is it a gullible spot?"

I twisted back. "Do you think that's it?"

A frown creased Emily's face. "You mean why he talked more to me about fairies?"

"Never mind." I shooed the question with a wave of my hand, trying to make light of it. "I miss him already. I'd listen to him talk about anything right now."

"I wonder when his son will get here. If he does."

"He's Ray's only child, and since he lives in California, it may be awhile."

"They have things called planes. They shuttle people quickly."

"He'll have to sell this house," I said. "How's he going to move all this furniture? And Ray's books and all the food he collected?"

"There's not really that much," Emily said, giving the living room another scan. "He didn't live a cluttered life, that's for sure."

"Selling the house," I mumbled absentmindedly. It struck me then that Ray might have considered moving before. I went back to the desk drawer. "There are two letters from Central Maine Realty here," I said. "I'm going to take a chance touching them." Quickly as I could, I slipped the letters from their envelopes, read them, and stuck them back in.

"Was Ray selling his house?" Emily asked.

"This realtor, Sheila Abbottson, was urging him to," I replied. "Reading the second of the two letters, she wasn't having much success."

"I can't believe how neat his place is. Any realtor would love it."

My eyes shot back to the desk, and from the desk to the couch and the console table behind the couch. "Emily, something is wrong. Did you touch the drawer in that other end table?"

"No yet."

"It's open slightly. Ray hated open drawers and cabinets. He said they looked sloppy. And look at the bookshelves."

"I didn't touch anything there," Emily said.

"He used to line up the spines, creating one neat line. And look at the console table. He never kept his address book on that, but it's there now."

"Oh, I see."

I swung back to the desk. "And the lid on that box of typing paper is askew." I strode up to the typewriter and flipped open the lid that covered the ribbon cartridge, again using my jacket to keep from leaving fingerprints. "There's no ribbon cartridge in here. There's a new one in his desk, but the one he was using is gone." Taking a quick peek at the empty trash bin next to the desk, I said, "No cartridge in here."

"Let me check the trash by the fridge," Emily said, moving for the kitchen.

Lost in thought, I looked down at the empty slot in the typewriter where a cartridge should have been. By the time I heard the front door open, it was too late to run.

CHAPTER 7

Fishing through the enormous tote bag she carried, the woman at the door didn't see me at first. She fished, kicked the door closed, and fished some more. When she looked up, she gasped and flinched—not in fear, it seemed to me, but in dismay at having been discovered entering the house. Her dismay grew when she saw Emily enter from the kitchen.

Yet the woman quickly recovered, and her dismay turned to belligerence. "What are you two doing in here? You have no business in Mr. Landry's house. I'll call the police."

I held up my key ring. "Go right ahead. We're neighbors with a key to Ray's door. Who are *you?*"

"Oh." The woman's shoulders relaxed and dropped an inch or so. "I see. Well, I didn't know anyone would be here. I'm basically responsible for maintaining this house. Or keeping it presentable and making sure it's locked up."

It was clear the woman was calculating how to present herself in the best of lights—and explain what she was doing in the house—and was coming up fairly empty-handed. "I'm Kate Brewer and this is Emily MacKenzie. And you are?"

"Sheila Abbottson. I'm Mr. Landry's realtor." She held up her own key ring. "And I have a key too."

"Realtor? But Ray wasn't selling his house."

"No, not that Mr. Landry." Sheila, along with her giant tote, sat on the couch. "His son, Owen Landry. He hired me to sell his father's house. Of course, I had to drop by and see what needs to be done before it goes on the market."

"When will that be?"

"As soon as possible." Sheila glanced about the living room, pursing her red lips in satisfaction. "It's not in bad shape at all. That's always a relief in these situations. You never quite know what you're going to encounter with an elderly person's house or how much you're going to have to spend before you can list a home. Then again, I haven't seen the rest of the house. It might well be one of these situations."

She was about forty-five, I thought, with shoulder-length reddish brown hair and large but deep-set hazel eyes. As she spoke, her eyes widened and eyebrows arched, giving her a look of frozen astonishment.

"Owen moved awfully fast," I said. "Ray's been dead less than twenty-four hours." I cringed inwardly as soon as the words left my mouth. Owen and his realtor were none of my business. But honestly, Sheila was already irritating me. *An elderly person's house.* Say his name, Sheila. *These situations.* What situations? Like murder? The woman was a vulture, circling and then swooping in, relieved she wouldn't have to waste money on sprucing up Ray's house. *Ray's house.*

"There's more to this than you know, Kate. How long have you been Ray's neighbor?"

I pulled out the desk chair and sat. Emily remained standing, legs planted, arms folded over her chest. She didn't like Sheila either.

"More than twenty years," I said. What's with Owen? I wondered. He couldn't have waited twenty-four hours before contacting this woman? What kind of son had he been to Ray? "Ray was a good man. He was well liked, and he loved his house and his land."

"He loved them a little too much, I think. He should have sold this place while he was still in his seventies."

"Why? He was perfectly capable."

Sheila clucked and displayed her concern with a condescending tilt of her head. "He had dementia, you know."

"Ray Landry?" I couldn't help but laugh. "He was as sharp as they come."

"Of and on, yes. But that's how it is with dementia. In the early stages it comes and goes. With Ray, it was getting worse."

"That's not true. Who told you that?"

"Owen was worried about him."

"So Owen told you that?"

"He pleaded with Ray to sell this house a year ago and move to a facility where he could have care when he needed it. As I said, there's more to this than you know."

"Is that why you wrote Ray? You wanted him to list his house?"

The already-arched eyebrows rose higher. "He spoke to you about that?"

Not wanting Sheila to know I'd been looking through Ray's mail, though she would probably find out soon enough, I ignored the question and stood to leave.

There was nothing more to be discovered in Ray's house, not with a realtor prowling around. "Can I ask you a favor? Ray stored his foraging finds in Ball jars in the kitchen. If Owen doesn't want them, I'd like to have them. I know some people in the neighborhood who would like the jars as keepsakes, and I don't think Ray would want his foraging to go to waste."

"What's a foraging find? You're not talking about bugs, are you?"

"Plants, nuts, berries."

"Oh, *that* foraging. Lawn food is not my idea of delicious." Sheila left her tote behind and strode for the kitchen, smoothing invisible wrinkles in her black skirt as she walked.

"There are about thirty jars," I said, trailing behind her.

On first sight of the jars, Sheila stopped abruptly. "Good gravy! I've never seen these before."

"You've never been in the kitchen before?" I circled around her and stood near the table.

"No, just in—" Sheila clamped her mouth shut.

"Just in?"

"Listen, I can almost guarantee Owen doesn't want any of the jars, but I'll check with him and let you know. Or one of us will. You can pick them up then. But please, take *all* of them with you at the same time. Otherwise, what gets left behind will have to go in the trash. Now I'll have to hire someone to take care of all this."

"Ray loved to forage," I said. "He said it kept him active and healthy, and I believe it did."

"I so hope these things are the last surprise I find." Still gazing in horror at the jars—I mean, for crying out loud, they were *jars*—Sheila shook her head, no doubt wondering if her dreams of a speedy sale were in jeopardy. "Owen didn't mention anything like this. He said everything was shipshape."

Emily jumped in. "It is. It's spotless." Her arms still wrapped across her chest, she joined us in the kitchen. "Is Owen flying in, I would hope?"

"Yes. He's arriving the day after tomorrow." Sheila made a snappy, soldier-like pivot in my direction and again fussily smoothed her skirt. "That means I've got to get to work. There's so much to do. People to hire, things to clean, paperwork to handle. Will you excuse me?"

Knowing very well that *Will you excuse me?* meant *Get out now*, I tugged at the hem of my jacket to make sure the folded pamphlet in my back pocket was hidden, and then headed for the door, pulling Emily with me.

"Just a second," Sheila said. "You didn't tell me what you two were doing in here."

"We wanted to make sure the police had locked things up," Emily said.

"I'm certain they did. They know what they're doing." She walked up to me and stuck out a manicured hand. "May I have your key?"

I had no right to tell her to leave, but that's what I wanted to do. *Get out of Ray's house. He wouldn't like you in here.* Instead, I gave her what I hoped she'd take as a semi-genuine smile and said, "I'll be happy to give it to Ray's son. I want to say hello to him anyway, and I can ask him about the jars at the same time so he doesn't have to call."

Sheila studied me for a moment, probably wondering if she could bully me into giving her the key.

Bur her version of bullying consisting of silently glaring, and that had no effect on me. "Well, that's it for now, then," she said at last. "Nice to meet you. I'll be sure to tell Owen we met. First thing."

Now *that* sounded like a threat. Never mind. Ray had talked about his son, and Owen had always sounded like a fine and decent man. If anything, he'd be pleased we were watching his father's house.

"Nice to meet you too," I said. Emily remained silent, which was just as well.

We left the same way we came—out the back door and into the woods—and as we headed back to my house, I pondered what I'd seen in Ray's living room. On first glance, everything had looked orderly, just the way Ray liked it, but on further examination, too many things had been the tiniest bit awry. Just a speck off—like three misplaced notes in a five-minute song. But if you knew that song inside and out, you could hear those wrong notes, even if others didn't.

"I don't think we gained much," Emily said as we stood outside my back door.

"Oh yes we did." I opened the door slowly, letting it creak and grate as a warning to Minette.

"Laurence can fix that squeak when he comes back."

"Don't bother him. I can fix my own squeaky door. I'd better learn." Remembering the small pamphlet I'd smuggled from the house in my back pocket, I took it out, sat, and tossed it down on the kitchen table. "Someone searched Ray's house, and they tried very hard to make it look like they hadn't."

"Huh?" Emily sat across from me. "Do you mean

the police?"

"Nope. They wouldn't have been so careful. They wouldn't have tried to hide a search, and besides, why would they have searched the living room? They think Ray died of a heart attack in the kitchen."

Emily gave me a barely perceptible shake of her head. "I think I hate what I'm thinking."

"I think we're thinking the same thing."

"The person who killed Alana Williams killed Ray. And then he—or she—searched Ray's house."

"And I believe I know what they were looking for," I said.

CHAPTER 8

I showed Emily Ray's memoirs, specifically chapter 14, and reminded her of the missing ribbon cassette in Ray's typewriter. "When the killer couldn't find his manuscript, he took the cartridge, thinking he might be able to reconstruct what was typed. But Ray had moved on from the Alana Williamson murder," I said. "His last chapter was on Donna's death. He ended his story there."

"So whoever stole it could pull the ribbon out and read the memoirs?"

"Maybe. Unless the typewriter went over the ribbon more than once." I lifted a shoulder. "I don't know, and the killer probably doesn't either, but he must have thought it worth a try. I remember reading a book about a spy who did that. The thing is, that cartridge was gone. If Ray had taken it out, he would've put a new one in. The person who took it also searched Ray's house and wanted to keep people from reading his memoirs."

"Who else knew Ray was writing his memoirs?"

"I'll bet Welch and Rancourt did."

"Agreed. He talked to them one day before his death, and we don't like coincidences."

"So who did *they* talk to? And did Ray mention his memoirs to anyone else? How many people knew he was writing them?"

"What did he write about Alana that has her killer worried?" Emily asked. "The description of her body?"

"I need to finish that chapter. And one more thing— my laptop." I was up like a shot, bounding for the corner desk in my living room. I felt charged with energy, a peculiar sensation after months of grief and lethargy.

Unlike Ray's living-room desk, mine was a monument to moderate disorder. I wiped a stack of bills off my laptop, hit the On button, and took the computer to my couch while I waited for it to boot.

"First, I want to know if Marie St. Peter is still working for the Smithwell Police," I said. "She and Rancourt were the first law enforcement officers on the scene."

"What about looking up old issues of the paper?"

"We may as well. Though if I remember right, Ray offered more information on the crime than the paper ever did."

I navigated to the Smithwell Police Department's website and clicked on its Staff Directory link. "And there she is," I said, swiveling the laptop to give Emily a better look. St. Peter was about forty, I estimated. Her light brown hair was fixed so neatly behind her head that not one stray wisp grazed her temples. She wore a broad, dimpled smile and oval, wire-rimmed glasses that made her round face look rounder. "She's gone up in the world. According to Ray, she was a lowly officer six years ago. Now she's a sergeant."

While Emily read St. Peter's brief bio, I glanced furtively about my living room for Minette. Either she was hiding or she'd left the house. I hoped the latter.

61

"And here's Rancourt," Emily said, angling the laptop my way. "Sixty, would you say? Maybe older. He's pretty gray. And kind of grizzled looking."

I had to agree with the grizzled part. Rancourt had the kind of face that declared he'd been through a lot, worked long hours, and seen too much of the bad side of life.

Emily whipped the laptop back her way. "OK if I use your credit card to access articles at the library? It's five dollars."

"Go for it." I gave Emily my credit card then went to my kitchen to make yet another cup of almond tea and give that pamphlet I'd found a look. At the hutch, thinking I might find a sleeping Minette, I stood on tiptoe and peeked inside the teacups on the uppermost of the two shelves. She wasn't there. But there was no need for concern, I told myself. She had taken care of herself long before she'd met me, and even before she'd met Ray.

As the kettle heated, I sat at the table and turned to the first page of the pamphlet—an author's bio. According to the bio, Irene Carrick was a local woman and a member of the Smithwell Garden Society. It was a strange topic for a gardening club publication, I thought. *Fairy Lore and Horticulture in Smithwell*. I wasn't even sure what that meant. How were the two connected? Had the society shelled out money for the publication?

The next page contained a short dedication to Foley's Nursery, which didn't surprise me. I'd purchased my rhododendron there. For a town of six thousand, Smithwell was blessed to have such a nursery. It had as large a selection of plants as any nursery or garden center in Bangor or even Portland, and it drew people from as far east as Dover-Foxcroft and as far west as Farmington.

Noticing a fold in one of the pages, I turned there. Ray had written the words "Paphiopedilum Maudiae" in the margin, and under those words, "Expensive. $32. But worth it." Ray, a man whose motto was "Use it up, wear it out, make it do, or do without," never spent thirty-two dollars on anything but groceries, and even then he expected three bags' worth at that price. So what on earth was worth three bags of groceries?

Fifteen minutes later, downing the last of my tea, Emily still toiling away in the living room, I was beginning to think that either Irene Carrick believed in fairies—which made me wonder what her fellow club members thought about her foray into fantasy land at the club's expense—or, as the title suggested, she knew a thing or two about fairy folklore and found the subject fascinating. The horticulture part of the title became clear in the pamphlet's last three pages, which listed places fairies were known to frequent, like pine forests and cottage gardens, and plants fairies were known to like.

It was in this latter section that Ray had scribbled more notes. Next to "Asters" and "Salvias," he had written "No," alongside "Dandelions" was the word "Sometimes," and just above a list of orchids, he had jotted "Always," underlining it twice. I ran my finger down the list. There it was, five orchids down: Paphiopedilum Maudiae. So the mysterious and expensive plant was a fairy favorite.

Had Minette asked him to buy it? Is that why Ray had written "worth it" in the margin? But I was getting too far afield of my purpose. "Anything interesting in the articles?" I called out.

"Oh yeah." A moment later Emily popped her head into the kitchen. "And I now have a list of suspects." She sat with me at the table and waved a piece of notepaper. "Rancourt and St. Peter, for starters."

"Stands to reason," I said, nodding my assent.

"Town Manager Conner Welch, since he was talking to Rancourt in the supermarket."

"Yup."

"Get this. Nick Foley, owner of Foley's Nursery."

"Why Nick?"

"He was questioned by the police because he was the last person to see Alana outside the school. She was at his nursery the morning of the day she died. He said she was buying a fern for her apartment."

"That's peculiar."

"I'll say. Then there's a local writer named Irene Carrick."

My mouth dropped open. "Good heavens. She wrote the pamphlet I took from Ray's house."

"That's not all. They also questioned—are you ready?—Sheila Abbottson, our chirpy neighborhood realtor."

My mouth hung open like an airplane hangar ready for a Boeing 707. "What did *she* have to do with it?"

"First, she's Welch's sister."

"Somehow I'm not surprised."

"Sheila was seen arguing with Alana the night before she died, and reading between the lines, it was a very personal argument. Not only that, but it got so nasty the police were called."

"Called where?"

Emily bent forward in her seat, eager to pass along

the next nugget of information. "To the Pumpkin Festival in Scarborough Park. Yipes! Can you believe it? What a place to have a fight. There must have been a dozen or more witnesses."

"What was the argument about?"

"The paper didn't say. The article writers danced around a lot of subjects. I think they wanted to avoid being sued since the police hadn't named a suspect or even a person of interest. And you know what *that* means. Everyone the police questioned had an alibi."

"Either that or the police couldn't link them even marginally to the murder," I said.

"I'll ask around and find out about that argument. It'll be a snap. The same vendors are setting up this year's Pumpkin Festival right now, and Laurence helped some of them with some . . . issues. I'll drop his name."

I cleared the table of croissants and teacups. "While you're doing that, I'm going to pay Irene Carrick a visit, using that"—I tipped my head at the folklore pamphlet—"as a pretext. I'm hoping the Smithwell Garden Society will give me her phone number."

"What are you going to ask her?"

I gently set the cups in the sink. *An excellent question, Emily.* "I don't have the foggiest idea," I said, turning around. "I'll wing it, depending on what she says. I'm hoping she's the talkative sort."

Emily scooped up Ray's memoirs. "I'm going to finish reading this before I go. Mind if I stay here?"

"Of course not." My thoughts took a sudden turn as I envisioned the thief-slash-killer still hunting for Ray's manuscript. And hunt he or she would, knowing that Ray would have given his story to a friend to read. It was simple deduction. "Emily, take the memoirs with you when you go, and keep them with you. That's the only copy. We can't lose it."

It dawned on Emily—I could see it on her face—that I was now worried about the killer breaking into my house or hers. "When we start asking questions around town, it'll become obvious that one of us has the memoirs," she said.

"We should find a place to hide it. Like a safety deposit box. Or we can make copies."

"Actually, Kate, I was thinking about *us*. We need to be careful. The person we're searching for has already killed two people."

"And one of them was the sweetest man I've ever known, aside from Michael. I'm not going to sit back and wait for a bumbling police force—or worse, a corrupt and involved one—to solve his murder." I had a purpose now, and the strength and stamina to fulfill it. For the first time since Michael's death. Danger or not, I was going to find Ray's killer. "I need to do this, Emily, but I'll understand completely if you don't want to."

"Hello? Did I say that?" She shook her head at me and clucked her tongue. "All I'm saying is let's be careful. You don't get to do this on your own. Got it?"

"Good," I said, heaving a sigh of relief, "because I really don't want to."

Memoirs in hand, Emily started for my front door. "Change of plans," she called over her shoulder. "I'm going to copy this whole thing first, then I'm going to finish reading chapter 14 in my car, and then I'm heading to the Pumpkin Festival grounds. You go do your thing with this Irene Carrick."

"Change of plans for me too," I said, catching up with her at the door. "First I'm going to visit Nick Foley. Irene dedicated her pamphlet to his nursery, so maybe he can give me her phone number. I'll buy something and ask him about it, get the ball rolling."

"Get a fern," she said. "That's what Alana bought the day she died."

"Maybe not," I replied. "I was thinking more along the lines of an orchid."

CHAPTER 9

I climbed into my Jeep, hit the remote on the garage door, and backed up down my drive until I came to a fat turn-around Michael had dug not long after we'd moved into our house—after I'd slid backward on ice, from the top of the long, sloping driveway almost all the way to Birch Street.

Half a mile down Birch, I made a right onto the Bog Road and pressed down on the accelerator, anxious to make it to Foley's. I rolled the window down a bit and took in the October air, smelling of woodsmoke and grasses dampened by the previous night's rain. The sparsely traveled stretch of road was hemmed in by trees two weeks past their full autumn glory and old utility poles, and here and there were aging white or gray clapboard houses and small stores and gas stations called, in deference to geography, Central Maine This or Central Maine That.

Shortly after I passed under the Bog Road's old train trestle, I turned west onto Route 2, and half a mile later, I was at Foley's.

I tucked my purse under the passenger seat, headed into the retail section of the nursery, and quickly spotted Nick Foley unloading heavy-looking bags from a rolling cart onto a shelf. He saw me, too, and raised his chin in a greeting as I walked over. A big, muscular man in his late thirties, he tossed five more bags to the shelves in the few seconds it took me to reach him.

"Compost," he said, nodding at the cart. His hands were nearly black with the soil, and his sweaty forehead was smudged with it. "People want to dress their gardens in the fall to get a head start on next year."

"Maybe I should do that," I said. "I didn't put any compost around that rhododendron I just bought."

"Top dress it," Nick said. "It'll do a world of good by next spring." He tore a foot-long piece of tape from a dispenser tied to the cart handle and patched a tear in one of the bags. Little wonder his hands were so dirty; several the bags were ripped and dribbling compost.

As far as I was concerned, I had laid the groundwork and performed the preliminaries, and it was time to talk about Ray. "Did you hear about Ray Landry?"

"Yeah. Shoot." Nick stopped unloading bags and wiped the sweat from his brow, leaving behind another soil smudge. He was beginning to look like he'd been down in the mines. "It's hard to believe. I thought that old-timer would outlast us all."

"The police think he ate bad mushrooms and had a heart attack."

Nick raised a quizzical eyebrow. "You mean mushrooms from foraging?"

"Have you ever heard anything so ridiculous?"

"Ray didn't pick bad anything." He pushed back a lock of brown hair with his dirty hand. "He taught a class on foraging—and took the class on an outing—a few years back."

"I didn't know that."

"We met here, then trekked into the woods. He pointed out the things you shouldn't touch, and not just mushrooms but all kinds of nuts and roots and things. He knew his stuff better than anyone I've ever met."

"I tried to tell the police that."

"Ray would have known if any mushrooms were bad. Bet on it." Nick rubbed the dirt from his hands then brushed his fingers on his dirty jeans. "But he could've had a heart attack. He wasn't a young man."

It was time to go for it, lay it out there, and see what sort of reaction I got. "He didn't have a heart attack," I said in a low, stern voice. "I think he was murdered."

My sharp shift in tone was matched by an equally sharp shift in Nick's body language. His head jerked and he folded his arms about his chest. "Ray? Who would want to kill Ray Landry? Everyone liked him. He lived in Smithwell his whole life, and he never had an enemy as far as I know."

"Well, he made one, and I think I know why." With Nick being on Emily's suspect list, it was a risky move to take, but the subject of Alana Williams wasn't going to raise itself. "He was writing about the Alana Williams murder six years ago."

A frown crossed Nick's face.

"Ray found her body and called the police. He was writing his memoirs, and he wanted to put down in black and white what he remembered from that day."

"It broke Ray up." Nick began to rub his right arm with the fingers of his left hand, like a child trying to comfort himself. "I've always wondered if he ever got over the trauma of it. Guess he didn't."

"He was over it, Nick. All he was doing was writing down what he remembered. That's what you do in memoirs."

"And did he remember?"

"He never forgot."

"What good did it do him, dredging all that up?"

"It bothered him that no one was ever charged, though according to the papers, the police questioned a few people."

"Yeah, they did." Nick tossed the last four compost bags to a shelf. "And my hunch is you know I was one of them." He straightened, looking at me with a mixture of disappointment and disdain.

Nick's change in demeanor was a red flag, and I should have been cautious, but ignoring my growing unease, I pressed on. "Can you tell me anything about Alana's death?"

"That was a terrible period in a lot of people's lives. I'd hate to see it start up all over again."

"Regardless of what you want, it *has* started up again. Except for her students and fellow teachers, you were the last person to see Alana alive."

"I told the police. She came in to buy a fern that morning. We said hello because I talk to all my customers if I can."

"Did she take the fern to school with her?"

"How should I know?"

"She must have bought it just before classes started. I wonder why she didn't wait until after school or the weekend."

"I wish I could help you," he answered, spreading

his hands. "But I don't know what to say. I didn't ask her what she was going to do with it."

"You must have wondered why she stopped by first thing in the morning for a fern."

"No, I didn't. I never have."

"But—"

"Leave it alone, Kate. Know what I mean?"

A tingle crept down my spine. "Someone murdered Ray Landry. One of the best men I've ever known. Don't ask me to leave it alone."

"Take it to the police."

"The same police who couldn't solve Alana's murder? Who think Ray ate bad mushrooms?"

"Then go buy another rhododendron. Gardening, Kate. It's good for all kinds of ills."

"You sell orchids, don't you?"

"Huh?"

He looked at me as though I'd lost my mind. In a way, I couldn't blame him. I was changing subjects faster than Minette could fly. "I just wanted to see your orchids. I might get one."

"Any kind in particular you're interested in? They all have different needs." He began to chew on his lower lip.

"No, I think I'll just browse, read the tags, and learn as I go."

As if realizing he was betraying his emotions, he stopped chewing and fixed a smile on his face. "Head back that way." He jabbed a thumb over his shoulder. "Almost to the rear of the greenhouse. Let me know if you have any questions."

At that he grabbed the cart, wrenched it around, and

made for the front of the garden center, up by the cash registers. The man couldn't leave fast enough.

I walked for the back of the greenhouse, threading my way through a maze of long tables toward the orchids. Fifteen feet away, I spotted them—I knew enough to recognize common orchid flowers—but before I reached the table, another display brought me to a halt. The sign on the table read "Fairy Gardens."

I'd heard of fairy gardens, of course. Those wide, shallow pots crammed with tiny plants, miniature garden implements, and little houses, fences, and stone paths. Lilliputian creations meant to suggest fairy homes and gardens—or what humans imagined such to be.

There were twenty or so pots on the table, and every single one held an exquisitely detailed garden, some of them complete with fairy figurines. Some of the figurines looked like cherubs, others like cartoon figures, but one of them was different. It was four inches high, intricately made, with wings like butterfly wings. I was about to pick it up when a woman appeared at my elbow.

"Aren't they pretty?" she said.

I nodded in agreement. "Beautiful. How do you know what to put in the gardens?"

"Oh, anything small will work. Alpine plants are good. You can make your own fairy garden if you'd rather choose what to put in it." She pointed at another table. "We have pots, pebbles, miniature paving stones, benches, and so forth, and on the next table some plant suggestions."

"What about orchids?"

She smiled. "Orchids are perfect. Especially the mini varieties."

"Everything keeps coming back to fairies," I said under my breath. A sentiment I never imagined I'd think, let alone utter in public.

"Excuse me?"

I grinned—idiotically, I'm sure—told her I was just thinking out loud, and headed for the orchids. What was I doing here? What was my life turning into? What if Ray had indeed died of a heart attack and I was indeed losing my tenuous hold on reality?

Now that I was at the orchids, I could see that fewer than half of them were in bloom. "Phalaenopsis Nemo," "Dendrobium Nobile"—their names were as enchanting as their foliage and flowers. I scanned the table until I found it: "Paphiopedilum Maudiae," thirty-two dollars. And it was in bloom.

The orchid's single flower was lime green and creamy white, and its leaves were a mottled green. My head was telling me to leave it on the table, but my heart was telling me to take it home.

I picked it up.

The woman at the cash registered cooed when she saw my orchid—a "Paph," she called it, pronouncing it like *paff*—telling me I was lucky it was in bloom. Then she told me it was the second one she'd sold in a week, which, I gathered by the way she said it, was out of the ordinary.

"My friend Ray Landry wanted to buy one," I said. "Did you hear he died yesterday?"

"Sure I did." She pouted briefly, demonstrating her sorrow. "Everyone knew Ray. He was in here last week asking about orchids. He was thrilled to find our Paphs, but he didn't buy one. He said he wanted to think it over.

74

He and that gardening writer came in looking specifically for it."

"The gardening writer?"

"That woman. What's her name? You wouldn't think it, but she loves orchids. She looks like more of a lilac kind of person." She tilted back her head, rummaging through her memories. "What's her name again?" She snapped her fingers and lowered her head. "Yeah, that's it. Irene Carrick."

CHAPTER 10

After a little coaxing, I'd prevailed upon the cashier, who knew Irene Carrick from the Smithwell Garden Society, to look up her phone number and dial it for me. "Tell her I need to talk to her about Ray Landry and orchids," I'd said.

Irene had readily agreed to meet me at her house. An "old white clapboard you can't see from the road for all the trees," was how she'd described it. There was no mailbox or number marker, so I was to drive north on Whitcomb Hill Road until I saw an asphalt driveway flanked by two six-foot spans of green fence with a chain stretched between them.

Carefully wedging my orchid between the back of the passenger seat and my purse, I drove off, glad that Irene was willing to talk to me but wondering how much I should tell *her*. I'd driven less than a mile when my phone rang. Seeing it was Emily, I pulled to the side of the road and answered.

On the off chance that the police had news on Ray, Emily had just called the Smithwell station. Certain that Ray had been careless and eaten foraged poison mushrooms, the detective in charge had encouraged the medical examiner to test the mushrooms in Ray's soup.

76

But the mushrooms were harmless. Ray's death was being ruled a homicide.

"Detective Rancourt wouldn't give me any details," Emily said. "When I asked him if neighbors should be worried, he said there were no signs of a struggle or break-in at Ray's house. That's it. Then I asked what made him call Ray's death a homicide, and he clammed up. The guy's not giving out any information."

"At least they recognize Ray was murdered," I said.

I hung up and continued to Irene's house, by some miracle spotting her green fence and chain in a stretch of Whitcomb Hill thick with pines. Irene was right about her house not being visible from the road. It wasn't until I'd gone a hundred feet up her drive—wondering all the while if it *was* her drive—that I broke through the trees.

When I pulled up to the house, a white-haired woman rose from a rocker. Even with the sun out and the rain long past, she wore a yellow slicker over her jeans. Another woman, maybe a few years younger, remained seated in another rocker, and she too was dressed for a rainy October day.

I got out of my Jeep and walked to the porch steps. "Irene Carrick?"

The woman slipped off her glasses, letting them dangle around her neck from a beaded chain. She was twenty-five years older and two inches shorter than me, with slender arms and toothpick legs, yet somehow she didn't give the impression of being frail. "You're at the right place. You're Kate?"

"Yes. Thanks for meeting me."

"If this is about Ray, I've been wanting to talk to someone who knew him. Come on inside. Mind the jack-o-lanterns. This is Norma Howard from the Smithwell Garden Society."

"Hello, there," the woman said in a throaty voice.

I sidestepped a number of carved pumpkins on the steps and by the door and followed the women to the kitchen, taking a seat at the table with Norma while Irene turned to the task of making tea. The room felt ice-box cold, so I kept my jacket on, as did Norma and Irene.

"I don't use teabags," Irene said. She looked back at the table as if challenging me to argue with her.

"Neither do I," I replied. "Loose leaf only, unless I'm in a rush."

"Capital. We'll get along fine."

While she waited for the kettle to boil, she joined me and Norma, and before I could tell her Emily's news about Ray, she said, "I knew that man for thirty-two years. As long as I've lived in Smithwell. Everyone knew him. Word's spread in town that he ate bad mushrooms in a soup and that's what killed him."

"Beyond ridiculous," Norma said, lacing her short, fleshy fingers together.

"What have you heard, Kate?" Irene asked.

I told her what Emily had told me—that the police had sense enough to declare Ray's death a homicide. "But they haven't issued an official cause of death yet. They won't say how he died, only that there were no signs of a struggle or break-in at his house."

"I don't understand it," Norma said. "Number one, Ray Landry was a gentle and kind man."

"I agree," I said.

"Number two," Norma continued, "he didn't have any enemies. Never did in all his years. He never made a single enemy in this town or state." She shook her head vehemently, puckering her lips as if to say, *And that settles the matter.*

"Norma thinks you can't make brand-spanking-new enemies and not even know it," Irene said. She pulled a handkerchief from her pocket and wiped her glasses before putting them on. "Mugs fine for you? I don't have fancy teacups. They only end up broken. A waste of money."

"Yes, fine," I said.

By the time Irene had pulled mugs from a cabinet and put milk and a bowl of lemon slices on the table, the kettle was boiling. She spooned tea leaves into a blue pot, poured the water, and brought the pot and a strainer to the table.

"I suppose you have fancy teacups," Irene said, looking askance at me as though I'd already answered in the affirmative.

"I do like my china," I said. "I have some Wedgwood I inherited from my mother, and my husband bought me several beautiful teapots. My favorite has an amazing purple vinca design."

"A veritable collection," she said.

"With Irene, one of everything will do," Norma said. "Not two, one. Even if it's cracked like this old pot she's had forever. The only reason she has enough mugs for guests is because I gave them to her." Norma nudged Irene with her elbow and Irene, properly brought down to earth, laughed.

"What can I tell you?" Irene said. "I'm an old Mainer."

"Lots of old Mainers have collections," Norma said.

"Can I pour?" She latched on to the blue teapot and filled all three mugs, pouring tea through the strainer.

"You're not from Maine, are you, Kate?" Irene asked.

How did she know? "Ohio originally. But I've lived in Maine for more than twenty years."

"And your husband buys you teapots," Irene said, taking one of the mugs. "Lucky you. By the time you're my age, you'll have a *real* collection."

I nodded and took a sip of tea. I didn't like discussing Michael with strangers, but I also didn't like pretending he was still alive, which Irene clearly thought he was. "He died ten months ago."

The mug halfway to her lips, Irene froze for a fraction of a second. "My large mouth," she said. "I place my foot in it on a regular basis."

"No, not at all," I said. "How were you to know?"

"But you're so young," Norma said.

"Am I?"

"What happened to him?" Irene said. "If I may ask."

I had the feeling Irene asked what she wanted to, when she wanted to. She was a bit of a bulldozer. "He died of cancer."

"That's a bad one. That took my Jack."

"I'm so sorry."

"It's been seven years. But how about you? Ten months isn't long."

I nodded, a little embarrassed that the conversation had so rapidly turned to me and Michael. "I'll be fine. What I want to do right now is find out what happened to Ray."

"I'd like to find that out myself," Irene said. "That's

why I wanted you out here, sight unseen. That man had ten more years in him, if you ask me."

"But who would want to hurt him?" Norma said, wearing a puzzled expression as she cradled her mug.

I answered quickly, as if I had no doubt. "The same person who murdered Alana Williams six years ago."

Norma and Irene stopped drinking their tea and stared, waiting for me to explain myself.

I was taking a risk, telling strangers about Ray's memoirs and his concerns about Alana's murder, but I spent the next few minutes filling Irene and Norma in on what I knew, leaving out my visit to his house and my conviction that it had been searched. "It's clear to me that Alana's killer believed Ray was getting close to something that would solve the case," I went on. I hastily added, "Though I haven't a clue what that might be."

"Irene here was questioned by the police," Norma said in a goading tone.

"I have a feeling our visitor knows that," Irene said. "Correct, Kate?"

"May I ask why they questioned you?" I said.

"I offered my services."

"They didn't haul her in," Norma added.

Irene cleared her throat. "I let them know Alana was having an affair with Nick Foley, the owner of Foley's Nursery."

I think my eyes bugged out.

"It wasn't an affair in the truest sense," Irene went on, "since neither of them were married. Nick still isn't. They weren't cheating on their spouses, but oddly enough, they behaved as though they were."

"How did you know?" I asked.

"I saw them in Foley's Nursery more than once," Norma said. "All I'll say is that it was more than obvious what was going on. I couldn't bear the idea of going down to the station, so Irene spoke up for me and left my name out of it. I think the nursery was where they went for their"—she wiggled her fingers and looked to Irene for help—"what do you call it? Assignments?"

"Assignations. And they likely went any number of places, Norma. You just happened to see them there. They were trying to keep their relationship secret, though why is anyone's guess."

"Did you talk to Detective Rancourt?" I asked Irene.

"Only a few minutes. He wasn't terribly interested in what I had to offer. I think I was just a nosy old lady confirming what the police already knew."

"What did you think of him as a detective?"

"I wasn't impressed." She trained her eyes on me, locking them in place.

"He didn't take you seriously."

"I don't think he took the case seriously."

I took a long sip of tea and then kept my mouth firmly shut. I knew nothing about these ladies, so it wasn't wise to share *all* my fledging theories with them. I suspected Rancourt. Simple fact. Who was in a better position to get away with murder than the detective investigating it? When I set down my mug after the longest sip in the world, Irene was still watching me. Like a hawk.

I leaned back in my chair, affecting an ease I didn't feel. It was time to switch subjects. "Irene, the cashier at Foley's told me you were with Ray when he looked at an orchid. A Paph, she called it."

"So?" she replied. "What of it?"

Was Irene refreshingly candid or just rude? The more we talked, the more my opinion seesawed between the two. Or maybe, approaching seventy-five or eighty, she simply didn't care to waste time.

Norma pushed a strand of wispy gray hair behind one ear. "Did you buy an orchid? For a woman who won't buy a new teapot, you're throwing away a lot of money on plants."

"I've never bought an orchid," Irene said. "But they're fascinating plants. Of course I'm interested in them. And as you well know, almost all my plants come from cuttings and my own seeds."

I decided to go for it. Irene, growing testier by the minute, could throw me out of her house, but she'd probably thrown most of the people she knew out of her house at one time or another. "Ray owned your booklet on fairy lore in Smithwell, and I noticed that one of the plants you wrote about is the Paph orchid."

"Yes?"

She was a tough nut to crack. "I think Ray believed in fairies, and that's why he wanted the orchid."

Irene gave a humorless snort. "Oh, God rest his soul, but it's ridiculous. There are no such things."

"But you wrote a pamphlet about fairies," I said.

"Fairy *lore*, Kate." Irene stood and gathered our mugs, taking Norma's right out of her hands. "Ray liked to believe in many things," she said, setting the mugs in her sink. "I believe in what I can see. No more, no less."

"But what if that isn't all there is?" I asked.

Irene spun back. "Of course that's all there is. That's why we have eyes in our heads and a head on our shoulders."

CHAPTER 11

"Irene, what's got into you?" Norma said. "You're not rude like this. You're a little rude, but not like *this*."

Irene shot Norma a quick, pinched-lip smile before turning her eyes to me. "The subject bothers me. Ray . . ." She looked down at her fingers, examined her nails, and shrugged. "I worried about him. And not because I thought he'd pick the wrong mushrooms or end up murdered."

"Then why were you worried?" I asked.

When she sat again at the table, her words came tumbling out. "I worried about him living alone. Yes, I know, I live alone, but I wasn't seeing things, was I? And Ray was. He was becoming like a child—like a child having hallucinations, I should say. I imagined him wandering off on his own, getting lost—all sorts of things. Finally, I had to stop thinking about him or I couldn't sleep at night. He'd never bought orchids before, and all of a sudden he talked about buying an orchid he couldn't afford, and all because of my pamphlet. I'll tell you something else, and it breaks my heart to say." She rapped the table with her fist. "If he saw things that weren't there, I'm not sure his memory of Alana's murder scene can be trusted."

Intrigued, Norma leaned in. "What did he see that wasn't there?"

"He never told you?" Irene said. "He never talked about fairies?"

"Sure he did," Norma said with a grin, "but he never told me he saw them."

"Well, he told *me*," Irene said.

You could have heard a pin drop. Or a fairy's wings flutter.

"What? When?" Norma said. "Really? He was joking with you. He must have been. Ray did have a sense of humor. You're joking, aren't you?"

Irene lowered her head and stared at Norma over the top of her glasses. "Do I look like I'm joking?"

"Where did he see these fairies?" I asked.

"I don't know," Irene said. "The woods, I suppose. That's where he was most of the time. He never said exactly where. Does it matter?"

"No, I guess not." I was oddly cheered by the fact that Ray hadn't told Irene he'd seen these fairies in his own house or garden, and that he obviously hadn't mentioned Minette by name. A woman as no-nonsense as Irene might swing a shovel at one of the little creatures, thinking it was a flying mouse or giant bee. "He said *fairies*, plural?"

"He very distinctly used the plural," Irene said. "Why? What's got your curiosity piqued?"

"I wish I would have talked to him more, that's all."

"He didn't tell you he saw fairies?" Irene asked.

"Unfortunately, no."

"When I was young, I heard the Smithwell woods were full of fairies," Norma said, smiling at the memory.

"My grandmother used to tell me tales she heard from *her* grandmother. She told us about pixies too, who aren't as nice as fairies and prefer spruce trees to maple, birch, and cedar trees."

"Stories like that go a long way back," Irene said. "Hence my booklet on the subject. Ray said fairies loved this time of year. The autumn leaves, the nuts and berries and moss. Hiding in jack-o-lanterns."

"That's so sweet," Norma said.

"That's crazy," Irene countered.

"I lean more toward Norma's assessment," I said. It was time for me to leave. Strangely, I was enjoying Irene's company, but I wasn't interested in hearing more about Ray's delusions. "Thanks very much, ladies. I'd better get going."

Irene stood at the same time I did. "You're upset. I'm sorry I told you about Ray and fairies. Forget about all that. He was a good man, one of the best, and we'll miss him."

"No worries," I said. "I'm not shocked."

"I never could've imagined he saw fairies," Norma said. "But you know, sometimes I think . . ." Her words trailed off, and I sensed that she wasn't quite as convinced as Irene was that Ray was seeing things, though she wasn't willing to contradict her friend.

Not wanting to press Norma on the point, I said my goodbyes and headed out to my Jeep. I rolled down the driver-side window to let in the fresh air, maneuvered around, and drove back down the driveway for Whitcomb Hill Road. My orchid looked none the worse for wear, having sat in my car for the past two hours, but according to the plant's tag, this was a temperate orchid, not a

87

hothouse one, and it didn't like the heat.

In assessing Ray's critical faculties, Irene had lacked one crucial piece of information: Ray had indeed seen fairies. Or at least one fairy. And so her argument that Ray was losing it, that he saw things that weren't there and so had probably misremembered Alana's murder scene, didn't hold water.

The late afternoon sun flickered through the trees along the road, striking autumn leaves and setting them aglow. Mid-October was one of my favorite times of year, a balancing act between early October's leaf-peeping season and the end of all that lushness, signaled by November's arrival. By the middle of October, almost half the leaves had fallen in my part of Maine, but when it rained, as it often did, the trees' wet, black bark shone like slate, underscoring autumn's beauty.

The sight was intoxicating, but I didn't drive slowly, as I usually did. Irene was wrong about Ray's memory, and I didn't have a lot of time to prove it. Ray had told me that his father once said murder cases started to go cold in just twenty-four hours. In forty-eight hours, the likelihood of catching your killer plummeted like a boulder off a cliff.

"It's not going to happen, Ray," I said out loud. "Detective Rancourt or not. Emily and I are on this, and we're not giving up."

I drove for downtown Smithwell—my intention was to visit Town Manager Welch—wondering if I should also visit the police station. The police were public servants, and as such, they wouldn't mind me asking them about the death of my neighbor. So I told myself. And if I had enough gumption, I'd ask Detective Rancourt what he and Ray had disagreed about in Hannaford's. But at that moment, Welch was a less daunting figure than Rancourt, so it was Welch first.

I made a right onto Falmouth Street, Smithwell's main road. Downtown was a cluster of brick buildings end on end, occasionally a clapboard house-turned-office building in between, centered on Falmouth and the corners of four cross-streets: Essex, Front, Water, and Pleasant. Driving north, a magnificent brick church came into view, its tall, white steeple and clock tower looming over the lesser buildings of downtown. My own church was in a much less impressive structure, but the sight of this brick behemoth never failed to cheer me.

As I parked on Essex, just off the corner of Falmouth, a fine, hard rain began to fall. I rolled up my window and dashed down the sidewalk for the Town Office on the corner of Falmouth and Water. It was another imposing building, in a sense out of proportion for our small town: a three-story brick Colonial Revival structure with two Doric columns flanking the entrance. By the time I made it up the building's short flight of steps, I was soaking wet.

I jammed my fingers in my hair, shook out the rain, and then studied the directory sign in the lobby. In our town, it wasn't out of the question to pop in on the town manager, but my business with him was, well, none of my business. Unless I made it my business, which I resolved to do. I steeled myself, headed down the hall, and rapped on his open door.

Conner Welch looked up from his desk. "Yes?" he said in a gruff voice.

"Have you got a moment?" I stepped hesitantly into

his office.

"Um . . ." He glanced at his watch, furrowed his brow, and sighed, letting me know what a busy man he was and how gracious he was about to be, letting me enter his hallowed office. "A couple minutes, that's all."

I didn't like the man. I had never liked the man. He'd risen from selectman at thirty-eight to town manager at forty-two in last year's election. I hadn't voted for him, and I never would. But I smiled, pretended gratitude, gave him my name, and asked if I could sit.

"Go ahead. Just a couple minutes is all I've got." He leaned back in his chair and folded his arms across his wide and slightly plump body.

With that time limit pressing on me, I dove in. "Ray Landry was a good friend of mine. I'm sure you've heard about his death."

"Yes. It's very tragic."

"The police ruled his death a homicide."

"I heard. What can I do for you?"

"Ray told me he ran into you and Martin Rancourt at the Hannaford the day before he died."

"I remember."

"He was concerned about something—enough so that he spoke to me about it the next day."

"Is that right?

"He was surprised to hear you talking about the murder of Alana Williams with Detective Rancourt."

"Why was he surprised? It was a remarkable event in Smithwell. Another tragedy." He dropped his arms and leaned forward. "I'm sorry, but I must be missing your point. What's the question?"

I could play it safe and get zip in return or I could

risk telling Welch, who might have killed Alana and Ray, what I knew and possibly reap a dividend. I chose the risk. "Ray said that he and Rancourt had a disagreement over the case."

"What was that?"

He was going to play it dumb. "That's what I'm here to ask you. Ray said you were there when it happened."

He shrugged. "I don't remember. You can ask Detective Rancourt. The police station is right next door."

"The police questioned you and your sister, Sheila Abbottson, about the case."

"This was a long time ago."

Until that moment, I'd only guessed that the police had questioned Welch as well as his sister Sheila.

"Your sister was seen arguing with Alana."

Welch glanced out his office window, back to me, and then at the clock above his door. As he turned his head side to side, I noticed his almost nonexistent sideburns, freshly shaved to the top of his ears in an out-of-date style that I had never liked on anyone and liked even less on him. It was all there in his haircut. He was a boy, a brat. If we were lucky in Smithwell, he'd move on to state politics, loaded with little boys, and leave us alone.

"I just want to know what Ray heard Rancourt say that worried him."

"You'll have to ask *him*, Mrs. Brewer."

Admittedly, he had a fair point, but I'd hoped to avoid asking Rancourt that question. I stood, thanked him, and started for the door.

"And leave my sister out of whatever fascination

you have with the Williams murder," he added.
I kept walking.

CHAPTER 12

The rain had slowed by the time I left the town manager's office, but I still hurried to the police station next door, worried that Rancourt was about to clock out for the day. Before I reached the station's front desk, I saw the detective talking with Marie St. Peter, waving a folder about, looking as pressed for time as Welch had been. Suddenly I felt queasy, a sensation I put down to nerves and an empty stomach.

The moment St. Peter walked off, I steamed toward Rancourt. *No time like the present.* I caught up with him at his office door.

"Detective Rancourt?"

He wheeled back. "Yes?"

"My name is Kate Brewer. You talked to my neighbor, Emily MacKenzie, this morning about Ray Landry."

He answered me with a grunt and a chin nod.

"Can we talk a minute?" I asked.

Rancourt squinted, deepening the furrows in his crow's feet. "About?"

"About Ray Landry."

He eyed his desk, made a petulant sound—rather like air escaping a balloon—and gestured for me to enter.

His office was small but bright, thanks to a window on the outside wall, a large glass pane between his office and the rest of the station, and an ugly brass light fixture in the middle of his ceiling.

"Mrs. Brewer, you were interviewed by Officer Bouchard?" he asked.

He didn't offer me a seat, but I sat nonetheless, choosing a metal chair near his desk. I was afraid he'd hear my knees knocking if I remained standing. "Yes, I was. The night Ray died."

"Do you have any new information?" He plopped himself down in his nice, cushy leather chair and smoothed his tie.

"Possibly. I've talked to a few people. But I had a couple questions first."

"Oh yeah? All right." He pulled a notepad from an inside pocket of his gray suit jacket and flipped it open. He looked a little less grizzled in person, I thought, but still pummeled by the job. His body—average height, stout but not excessively fat—was fifty-five, but his face was ten years older, with black-green circles under his eyes and a pallor that suggested a bad diet.

"Can you tell me how Ray died?"

"He was suffocated."

I gasped. I hadn't expected Rancourt to be so forthcoming, and I hadn't pictured such a violent end for Ray. "Then why wasn't his death immediately ruled a homicide?"

"He was found at his kitchen table, and the suffocation wasn't apparent. He wasn't strangled."

"Then how—"

"That's all I can tell you."

"Could a woman have done it?"

Rancourt cocked his head and said nothing.

"Ray was eighty-one," I went on, "but he was pretty tough for that age. Though maybe not tough enough to combat a young, strong woman who took him by surprise. Maybe suffocated him with something while he sat at the kitchen table? I don't think a man or woman would have killed him elsewhere and then moved him to the kitchen. But you're not going to tell me, are you?"

"I'm sorry, I can't."

"He was my friend."

"I know that."

"He called 911 that night."

"Yes. And then he hung up, but we traced the call."

"The killer was already there. That's why he called. He made it to the phone but couldn't complete the call, and the killer forced him back to the table."

"That's a possibility."

"Did you know Ray was rethinking the Alana Williams murder?"

A shadow passed over Rancourt's face. "We talked about it last time I saw him."

"I know. He also said you two disagreed on some fact or facts of the case. It bothered him enough to tell me about it."

"It bothered him?" Rather than looking puzzled, Rancourt seemed pained. He sat a little straighter in his chair. "He was adamant. I couldn't talk him out of it."

Speaking slowly and distinctly, so he'd grasp my meaning, I said, "Ray Landry had a sharp memory. Crystal clear. And an eye for detail like no one I've ever known. He got it from his father, who was a cop."

95

I heard a rap on the doorframe and turned to see Marie St. Peter at the door, leaning in, waiting for Rancourt to signal she could enter.

"Sergeant?" he said.

"You wanted the toxicology, sir."

"Already? Since when do they move so fast?"

St. Peter smiled, strode to Rancourt's desk, and handed him the folder. "Since the Pumpkin Festival is tomorrow and they don't want this on their plate?"

"Ah yes, we must make time for pumpkins."

"And all things pumpkin spice, sir."

St. Peter looked my way, and as I judged her to be on the friendly side despite her severely drawn-back hair, I said, "Do you have a moment? Can we talk?"

"No you *cannot*," Rancourt said curtly. "We've got a murder to solve. You're welcome to come back when we've done our job. I'll be happy to talk to you then."

"Well, if you can't—"

"Thank you, and good day."

"But I—"

"*Good day*, Mrs. Brewer."

Fuming, I stormed out of his office and marched straight for the vending machine I'd seen by the building's front door. I stuck a couple bills in the slot, tugged on a knob, and retrieved the granola bar that plunked to the dispenser bay a second later. Angry as I was, I was also famished.

As I ate right there in the hall, I looked back to Rancourt's office. He was at work at his desk, and I couldn't be sure, but he seemed to be mumbling to himself. Either that or he was chewing gum.

A moment later St. Peter appeared from around the

corner, and seeing me, she halted. I stepped forward, keen to let her know I still wanted to talk, and for an instant I thought she might speak to me, but she appeared to think better of it. She glanced at Rancourt's office, shot me a terse smile, and moved on.

I trotted down the station steps and headed for my car. The rain had ended, leaving the asphalt on Falmouth glistening. As soon as I hopped into my Jeep, I got a call from Emily. She told me she'd left Ray's memoirs in my living room and, not to worry, she had made a copy and squirreled it away where no one nefarious would find it.

"I've got a meeting in an hour with someone who remembers the fight between Alana and Sheila Abbottson," she said. "See you at your house later tonight?"

"Sounds good. We'll put our clues together."

"By the way, I left a pumpkin in your dooryard. Got it from a vendor at the festival."

"Why?"

"So you can carve it, you goof. You used to love this time of year."

"Yeah, pumpkin spice everything," I said.

"What?"

"I'm thinking out loud. See you in a while, and we'll have more of your chocolate cake."

I drove home, thinking I hadn't learned much that day and wondering what I was going to whip up for dinner. I parked in my detached garage and crossed the driveway for my side door, carrying my orchid with me. Before entering my house, I glanced down at Emily's enormous pumpkin gift. No way was I carving that monster by myself.

Instantly I was alert for Minette. In the kitchen, I set the orchid on the table, slung my purse strap on the back of a chair, and zeroed in on the hutch. Nothing. I drew closer, and then I checked inside the teacups. More nothing.

Maybe the little creature had no intention of returning, I thought. We had met by accident, because of the rain and the pots, and she had probably taken off for the forest. Though I thought she'd enjoyed my company last night, and I *knew* she wanted me to find out who had killed Ray of the Forest. The relief was that I *wasn't* losing my mind. Minette was quite real. But though the burden of that worry had lifted, it saddened me to think I might never see her again.

I fixed myself a sandwich, ate quickly, then made a cup of tea and took it, my laptop, Ray's memoirs, and Irene's pamphlet into the living room, dropping with a sigh to my armchair by the fireplace. How many fall and winter evenings had Michael and I spent by the fire, reading and talking? And how was I going to make it through the rest of my life without hearing his voice again?

"Stop it right now," I said aloud. I set the laptop and teacup on the raised hearth and flipped to chapter 14 of Ray's memoirs. "I'm going to find out who did this to you, Ray. I promise with everything I have."

Seconds later I heard a faint scratching sound coming from the fireplace. I'd opened the damper a week ago to light a fire. Had I ever closed it again? The last thing I needed was a bird . . .

I leapt from my chair and sat on the raised hearth. "Minette?"

Silence. Then a flutter of wings. "Kate."

I was overjoyed—so much so that I almost knocked over my teacup. "Minette, come down here."

Feet first, she dropped slowly down from the flue into the firebox, hovering over the charred wood in the grate, her pink wings vibrating. Magically unscathed by soot, she smiled, flapped her wings forward, and flew horizontally into the living room, coming to a rest on Michael's armchair.

She watched me closely for a moment, a puzzled expression on her tiny face, then asked, "You're glad to see me?"

"Of course I am." I picked up Ray's manuscript from where it had fallen, laid it on the laptop, and sat in my chair. "So that's how you left the house. I was wondering."

"I didn't think you would be glad to see me."

"I'm sorry. I haven't reacted very well. But you have to realize, I was afraid. Humans don't think fairies exist."

"Because humans don't believe what they can't see."

I chuckled. "I met a woman today. Irene Carrick." I pointed at the pamphlet. "She wrote this booklet about fairies in Smithwell, but she doesn't believe in them." I leaned in for a better look at Minette, resting my elbows on my knees. The rose-petal wings that bore her like a flash of lightning when she went horizontal looked much too soft and dainty for the job, and her light brown hair, a mass of short, radiant waves, still shimmered, even in the low light of the living room. "Do you know why Ray didn't tell me he saw fairies? He told Irene. Not that it did any good. She thinks he was crazy."

"He was very careful who he told," Minette replied.

"I'm sure he was. I just thought he would have . . . well, I don't know. Never mind."

Minette half scooted and half fluttered her way to the edge of the chair. "You don't believe in things you don't see, Kate."

"Neither does Irene, it turns out."

"But she wrote that book. I think Ray of the Forest was fooled by that. He thought he could talk to her."

"Ray wanted to buy you an orchid, didn't he? Because Irene wrote about it?"

"I like orchids. Irene is right about them, but she's wrong about many other things."

"Including Ray."

Minette tilted her head at me. "Are you sad?"

The question caught me off guard. Did she mean about Ray? She couldn't have known about Michael, could she? Anyway, I was practiced at hiding my grief over Michael. Darn good at it, as a matter of fact. I had to be. After the first month, people didn't want to hear about your grief or your fears or death in general. It embarrassed them.

"I'm sad about Ray, Minette. I'm trying to see . . ."

"What do you see, Kate?"

I slumped back in my chair, shaking my head in frustration. "I'm not sure." I thought about my conversations with Welch, Rancourt, and Irene and remembered what I'd seen in Ray's house that morning. I pictured Ray's face again as he warned me not to trust anyone I didn't know. "I see . . ." I picked up his memoirs and flipped to chapter 14. "I see the sort of man who

100

would've told me what I needed to know. I see that he thought something might happen to him."

Minette squeaked and covered her mouth.

"I'm sorry, Minette. I see . . ." I looked down at Ray's memoirs, at his second handwritten note.

"Kate?"

"Coffee," I said. "That's it. I think I know what Ray meant."

CHAPTER 13

Stuffing my keys in my jeans pocket, I strode for my back door, intent on sneaking into Ray's house again—before Ray's son flew in from California.

"Where are you going?" Minette buzzed around my head like a freakishly huge pink bee as I slipped into my jacket.

"To Ray's house. I'll be back. Emily will be over soon, so you'll have to hide when you hear her. And don't fly in front of the windows."

Minette hovered in front of me, no more than a foot from my face. "I will go with you."

"You can't."

"I can."

"Stay here where it's safe."

Every time I made a move for the back door, she circled around me and hovered again, saying, "You can't stop me. I will go with you."

Her tiny, honeyed voice had turned fierce, and her lips were pursed in a tight, angry line. For a moment, the incongruity—that childlike face and that ferocity in one tiny being—was almost comical.

I gave in. "All right, Minette, but you have to keep yourself hidden. Your wings are pink. And I don't know if you realize it, but your eyes and hair glow a little."

"I know. Like fireflies." She dove headfirst for my right jacket pocket.

"Good heavens!"

"Do not put your hand in here."

"Umm . . ." I held my right hand up, well away from my pocket, and looked down to see Minette's face, the size of a dime, staring up at me. "Okay, I'll try not to."

"I will sit down. No one will see me."

"If you hear me talking to someone, don't poke your head out. Stay hiding no matter what."

"Yes, Kate."

"I should take a flashlight."

"No, turn on a light in the kitchen. A flashlight will put you in trouble."

"I guess a flashlight does look more suspicious."

As I had done with Emily, I cut through the woods behind my house until I reached Ray's back yard and then entered by his back door. I called out in the dark, and hearing nothing, I turned on his overhead kitchen light.

"It's safe for now," I said.

Minette flew out of my pocket with the same speed she had entered it and landed atop Ray's refrigerator. "Ray of the Forest," she said. She let out a small sob, catching it in her hands.

"I'm so sorry, Minette. I'll find out who killed him."

"But his jars are gone. Who took his jars?"

I wheeled back to the shelves where Ray had stored his Ball jars. Every single one of them was gone. All the foraging he'd done, all those jars he'd worked so hard to fill. "Sheila Abbottson! She promised to wait. It hasn't even been twenty-four hours."

I leaned against the counter, my emotions lurching from anger to grief. So that was it, then. Ray's life had been brutally taken, and now, everything he'd worked for and loved had been taken too—in a single day. What were they going to do next, rip out the carpet in his living room? Tear out the kitchen cabinets? Dig up the rhododendrons he and Donna planted twenty years ago?

"Ray of the Forest wouldn't mind so much, Kate. Not as much as you."

I gazed up at Minette. "I think he would. He worked hard on foraging and on those jars, and Sheila just tossed them."

"We miss him, but he's happy. He doesn't mind about jars."

"I'm glad you think so."

Minette dropped crossed-legged to the fridge. "You never, never believe in things you can't see."

"I believe in *you*."

"You *see* me."

"Point taken, score one for you. You're right, I don't believe in things I can't see. If that makes me a crazy person, so be it."

I knew I sounded angry, and truth be told, I was, but not at Minette. I was tired, hungry, and devastated over Ray's murder. Slowly, slowly it was sinking in that I would never see him again. And I was ticked off at Sheila and Nick and Welch and Rancourt and the whole scheming lot of them. Not to mention rightfully freaked out that I was having conversations with a fairy.

"That doesn't make you crazy," Minette said. "It makes you sad."

"Don't lecture me."

"No lecture." Minette bit her lower lip and continued to watch me intensely, unnerving me. How old was she? I wondered. She had the face of an eight-year-old but gave the impression of being a middle-aged know-it-all.

An awkward moment later, Minette said, "What does 'coffee' mean?"

"Yes, that's what we're here for," I said, rubbing my hands together. "When I visited Ray in the morning, he would make coffee for me, not tea. I didn't mind because I like coffee too, but he always asked me if I wanted sugar with my coffee because he loved mounds of it." I grabbed the canister labeled "Sugar" from his counter and popped the top open. "If I'm right, there's something in here he wants me to see. It's like the thrillers we loved to talk about—secret code, Minette. He wrote 'Coffee' because he knew I'd think of him putting sugar in his coffee. The police wouldn't know that, and his killer wouldn't know that."

As I tipped the canister and began to pour out the sugar, Minette flew from the refrigerator to the counter top. "There's something there," I said.

She squeaked with delight.

"A piece of paper," I said, digging my fingers into what was left of the sugar in the canister. I pulled out a half-sheet of lined notebook paper with a black-ink drawing on it.

"What is it? What?" Minette cried, her wings vibrating in my ears.

"A drawing of Alana Williamson. Minette, back off, *please*. I can't think when you do that."

Still hovering, she fluttered backward a foot.

105

"It's Ray's recollection of Alana in the woods, the day he found her," I went on. "We need to get out of here now."

To be certain I'd found everything, I emptied the rest of the canister on the counter and then quickly scooped the sugar back in. I brushed the last of it into my hand, dumped it down the sink, and set the canister back in place.

"Lights must go off now!" Minette ordered. "Someone is here."

I hit the light switch, seized the knob on the back door, and hesitated there, straining to hear what Minette had heard. "It's the driveway," I whispered.

Minette swooped into my jacket pocket and I raced out the back door, speeding for the woods. I'd forgotten to lock the door, but it was too late to go back.

It wasn't until I was inside my own back door and sitting at my kitchen table—Minette out of my pocket and perched on my hutch—that I was able to catch my breath. "I wonder if that was Owen. Do you think he came early?"

"He lives in California," Minette reminded me. "Why would he come at night?"

"Still, it might have been him. Or Sheila Abbottson. Or maybe it was Rancourt and St. Peter, now that they've called his death a homicide. They have to go back over the house, if they haven't done that already. I didn't see any crime-scene tape, so either they haven't gone back or they've finished." I smoothed Ray's now-wrinkled drawing on my table, giving it a good look for the first time.

Above the sketch of Alana's body, Ray had written

106

"Rancourt's recollection."

"You must read the memoirs again and look at that drawing again," Minette said. She took to the air and landed on the table. "See what Ray of the Forest remembered that the chased rabbits did not."

"And that will be the answer to the question I've been asking myself since yesterday," I said, spellbound by the primitive drawing. Ray had drawn an arrow pointing at Alana's neck, and another one pointing at her long jacket. There was Alana's scarf—not wrapped around her neck but blown back, as Ray had written—the short-handled knife protruding from the right side of her neck, and her dress, which came just below her knees. Her jacket was unbuttoned, but it was much more askew than Ray had described it. And then . . . I leaned in.

"Minette, there's no heart necklace in this drawing. That's why Ray drew an arrow pointing to her neck."

"Someone took it after Ray of the Forest saw it."

"Yes, and Ray remembered Alana's jacket unbuttoned but neat. Not like this—wide open and sloppy. The killer left it neat—or if not the killer, someone else did. I wonder if Ray wrote 'Coffee' in his memoirs just before he gave the manuscript to me, and then made this drawing a couple hours later, when he thought something might happen to him. It looks like it was done very quickly."

"Someone is coming now," Minette said.

I was about to ask what she meant when the doorbell rang.

"How do you do that?" I said, getting to my feet. "I didn't hear anything until the bell rang."

"Fairies hear better than humans."

"They sure do. That's Emily, I think. I'm sorry, but you have to hide while she's here. I can't tell her about you. It's not that I don't trust her, but it's too soon to say anything."

"You must not tell," Minette said. She lifted off from the table, hovering an instant, her emerald eyes peering into mine.

"Where are you—"

Before I could finish, Minette went horizontal and took off in a blur for the living room.

CHAPTER 14

I tucked Ray's drawing in my jeans pocket and checked the peephole before I opened my front door. Emily looked about ready to burst with news. Grinning and holding up a quart jug of my favorite cranberry-apple drink—the one I went nuts for every October—she strode directly to my couch, pivoted, and dropped, one hand still on the jug. "Got glasses? I have fresh information."

"I have some of my own. You first, but hang on a sec."

I took down a couple glasses from a cabinet, went back to the living room, and sat at the opposite end of the couch, angling my body to face her. "You talk, I'll pour."

"That argument Sheila Abbottson was having with Alana the night before she died? It was about Nick Foley."

"No kidding?"

"Rebecca, the woman who sold me that cranmac, heard most of the argument. Okay, let me get this right," Emily said, her eyes momentarily lifting to the ceiling. "Sheila warned Alana to stay away from Nick. Rebecca remembers her saying something like, 'I'm dead serious. If you think I'm not, try me.'"

"That's creepy." I handed Emily a glass, poured my

109

own, and put the jug on the end table behind me.

"That's not all. Sheila accused Alana of playing games with Nick and ruining his future. Rebecca remembers that word—*ruining*. Sheila said she knew Alana wasn't serious about Nick and she was going to tell him that and make sure he broke it off with her."

"Good heavens. Was Sheila interested in Nick too?"

"She may have been interested in him, but how likely is it that her feelings were returned? Sheila's at least five years older than Nick, and Alana was twenty-four when she died. It's a sad fact of life that Alana had a much better shot at him. Nick was in his early or mid-thirties at the time."

"Something like that." I took a sip of my cranmac while trying and failing—thankfully—to imagine Sheila Abbottson dating Nick Foley. "Maybe they weren't talking about dating or love."

"Though it sounds like it was a leave-my-man-alone fight, and it was bad enough for the police to be called."

"It must have been wild. What else did you find out?"

"You first."

My news was terrible, but Emily had to know. "Ray was suffocated to death." The pain I'd suppressed since hearing of Ray's death rose to my throat, swelling it. I had to force my remaining words out. "Probably at his kitchen table, though Detective Rancourt wouldn't confirm that. That's *my* guess."

Emily grimaced. "How could someone do that? He was so kind and gentle. Suffocated. What was he suffocated with?"

"Rancourt wouldn't say. I was surprised he talked to

110

me at all."

Next I told Emily how strangely Nick, Conner Welch, and Irene Carrick had behaved when I'd questioned them. And how Rancourt, at first forthcoming, had started to shut down when I told him Ray disagreed with him on some facts of the case, and how he'd then thrown me out of his office when I asked to speak to Marie St. Peter. "I can't decide if he's hiding something or just being a good, closed-mouth detective. I also discovered something at Ray's house." I dug the drawing out of my pocket, unfolded it, and gave it to her.

"Where did you find this?"

"In Ray's sugar canister."

"Why on earth?" Emily glanced up at me.

"It's a long story. The important thing is, Ray used that drawing to illustrate how his recollection of Alana's murder scene differed from Detective Rancourt's. Look here," I said, tapping the arrows on the drawing. "Ray remembered a heart-shaped necklace, which is missing in this drawing. Rancourt must have claimed he never saw it. And Alana's jacket isn't as neat and smooth as when Ray saw it. They disagreed about those two things."

"Ray left this for you, Kate. You two and your crime thrillers—he knew you'd find it."

"Between the time Ray found Alana's body and the police arrived, who took the necklace? I see only three possibilities. The killer, the police, or someone lurking in the woods, like another forager. Ray felt he may have been watched, but . . ." I shook my head. "I think it was his nerves. I don't see the killer or a hiker or anyone else hanging around to steal from a murder victim."

"Do you think the necklace was a gift?" Emily

asked, handing back the drawing.

"I think we should ask Nick Foley that very thing," I replied. "Tomorrow morning. He got very nervous when I asked him about Alana. He even got nervous when I asked to see his orchids."

"Did you honestly buy one?"

"Sure."

"You? Since when are you interested in orchids?"

I lifted a shoulder and issued a noncommittal mumble. "Anyway, Irene said the same thing about Ray as Sheila did—that he was getting senile."

"What a load of baloney."

"And Norma, Irene's friend, thought it was possible he was getting dementia because he was—"

I put my hand to my mouth. I'd almost let it slip.

"What is it, Kate?"

How was I going to explain myself without giving up Ray's secret, and mine? I longed to tell Emily, the only person I could trust with such a revelation, but Minette's safety was paramount. So I fudged the truth. "Ray told them he believed in fairies."

"Oh, that's nothing. He told you and me that too. He told a lot of people that. It was his sweet imagination— and those fairyland woods across the street. Sometimes *I* think I can see fairies there."

"Emily, he told Irene he *saw* them. Really and truly saw them and talked to them."

"Oh." A second later, it sank in. "Ohhh."

"Irene was worried about Ray living alone. And by the way, I don't think she's our killer. She's got to be in her mid-seventies now, and I don't picture her winning a battle with Alana, or even smothering Ray. Besides, I think she cared for him a great deal."

"Wow."

Emily was still processing the seeing-fairies thing.

"Are you sure Ray wasn't kidding Irene?" she asked, brushing her short, coppery bangs from her forehead.

"Not according to Irene."

"He always had a twinkle in his eyes when he talked about fairies. I didn't realize he thought he saw them. Maybe he was a little, kind of, getting older."

My heart sank. "Not you too."

"You have to admit, it's a little out there."

Wanting to defend Ray, but knowing that for now I couldn't, I steered our conversation to the subject of Ray's memoirs. "Drink the rest of your cranmac," I said. "I need to finish chapter 14. Ray wrote more than the five or six paragraphs I've seen so far."

"When you've finished, you can give me a run-down. Where's this orchid?"

Thankfully, Minette had flown for the living room when Emily rang the doorbell, not settled herself inside one of my Wedgwood teacups. "It's in the kitchen, on the table."

Minette had probably whooshed up the flue again. Or maybe she was upstairs. I hoped the latter. I knew she could take care of herself, but now that Ray was gone, I felt responsible for her, almost as if Ray himself had placed that responsibility on my shoulders.

I turned to chapter 14 in Ray's memoirs and picked up where I'd stopped reading. "I believe the police focused on a man being the murderer," he wrote, "but I think that was shortsighted. There were no drag marks, as

I noted earlier. She wasn't dragged to the spot, which would have required more strength. Even the disturbed leaves I saw and thought at the time were signs of a small struggle, might have been disturbed only when Alana fell and made her final movements before dying. There was no way to tell. And anyone can wield a knife."

"Why was Alana in the woods to begin with?" Ray went on. "Who would she follow there? In reality, the answer is almost anyone. Ours was, and is, a small and friendly town. So Alana might have followed a man as well as a woman. I have also wondered about the murder weapon. I found from talking to someone two weeks later (he was not supposed to tell me this, so I will leave out his name) that short-handled knife had a long and thin blade. The murderer hit the carotid artery and she bled internally. The only good thing that can be said is that she died very quickly."

Emily emerged from the kitchen carrying her glass and my Paphiopedilum Maudiae. She placed the orchid on the table at her end of the couch and said, "It's such a delicate flower." Enthralled by its beautiful bloom, she ran her finger over its lower, pouch-like petal. "I can see why you bought it. Where are you going to keep it?"

"In the kitchen, probably. On the hutch. There's plenty of light, and it looks good with the cups and teapots." I went back to Ray's memoirs and read his final paragraph on Alana. "After writing this, I think I have found something I can do with my days. I have always enjoyed a good thriller with a good puzzle, and now I will turn my thoughts and efforts to the puzzle of Alana Williams's death. There's no better way to spend my time than trying to bring peace to Alana's loved ones. And if I can enlist the help of my thriller-loving neighbor, Kate Brewer, who knows what we may discover?"

Tears welling in my eyes, I set his manuscript on the couch next to me.

"Are you all right?" Emily asked me.

I nodded. "Let's go to Ray's house. Right now. I want to find out who drove up while I was there getting that drawing." I paused, checked momentarily by the look of apprehension on Emily's face. "You don't have to go, but I'm going. And I'm going to knock on the front door this time."

CHAPTER 15

As Emily downed the last of her cranmac, I grabbed my car keys in the kitchen and hurried back to the living room to listen briefly for Minette. She'd probably exited the flue, but not having seen or heard her for a little while, I was beginning to worry. The little creature had loved Ray, and I think in a funny way she had felt protective of him. I hoped she hadn't heard me talking about how he died. I had wanted to spare her that.

"Can't find your keys?" Emily said.

I wheeled back. "No, no. I've got them."

"Why are you so jumpy lately?"

"I'm not jumpy," I said, marching back into the kitchen and outside to the garage.

Emily and I climbed into my Jeep and I backed down the driveway until I hit the turnaround.

"I've known you for as long as you've lived next door," Emily said. "There's something you're not telling me."

"Why do you say that?" I maneuvered the Jeep around and drove for Birch Street, fighting to keep my voice and expression neutral.

"It's a very strong feeling. Don't avoid the question and don't tell me I'm imagining things, Kate Brewer."

116

Seconds later I swung right onto Ray's driveway. "They're tossing his things," I said.

"And don't change the subject."

"No, look." At the top of the driveway, feet away from Ray's front door, was a large brown dumpster, and next to it a small van. "At this hour?"

Making my way up the drive, I passed a car parked in the grass. I came to a stop behind the van just as a tall man wearing bib overalls was exiting the house, a wooden chair in each hand. He glanced up at me, hoisted the chairs chest-high, and then unceremoniously dropped them into the dumpster.

I strode through the open front door, ignoring the pointed stares of another man inside the house, and marched from the living room to the kitchen.

"Excuse me, ma'am."

I turned. The man who had stared at me in the living room was staring again, confusion lining his face.

"Are you with Central Maine Realty?" he asked me.

"No, I'm Kate Brewer. Who are you and what are you doing with Ray Landry's things?"

He frowned and pulled in his chin. "You mean the guy who lived here? Um, dumping 'em. That's what we were told to do."

I squeezed my eyes shut and took a deep breath. "First the Ball jars and now this."

"Yeah, those jars in the kitchen," the man said. "I'll bet you can get canning jars pretty cheap at Marden's."

I opened my eyes. Ray's jars were more than canning jars. Michael and I had helped him fill some of those jars. We'd picked and dried blueberries, raspberries, and garlic mustard for him as a thanks for teaching us to

117

forage. Those jars held memories.

"Sorry," the man said. "I didn't know anyone wanted them. We're doing what we were hired to do, that's all. And the realtor said they looked junky."

"Sheila Abbottson?"

"Yeah, she's the one. They're listing this house tomorrow afternoon. She's upstairs if you want to talk to her."

"Oh, you bet I do."

"I'm Carl, by the way."

"Sorry." I stuck out my hand. "I'm Kate, Ray's neighbor." I looked past him to where Emily was standing to one side of the door, trying to keep out of the other dumpster man's way. "There was a photo in a small frame on the console table in the living room. Please don't throw it out."

He twisted back. "If there's anything you want, just take it," he said with a sweep of his arm. "Please. It'll save us the work."

"What about Ray's son?" Emily asked. "Doesn't he want anything?"

"We've already boxed what he asked for. Mostly photo albums. I guess he can't ferry too much all the way back to California."

"So Sheila told you to *throw away* everything? What a waste."

"No, we're taking some things to the Salvation Army. That's why the van's out there."

On the console table behind the couch, I saw the photo I had taken of Ray and Michael in the woods, foraging for wild carrots. How I remembered that day two springs ago. Just a week earlier Michael had been

118

diagnosed with cancer, but he wouldn't say no to Ray's invitation to hunt the woods. He wouldn't give up. He never *did* give up—not until the last two weeks of his life. I ran my finger over the glass in the frame, wishing I could reach right through it—enter it—and touch him.

"This is the photo," I said. "I'm taking it out to my car."

"And I'm taking this." Emily snatched a watercolor painting from the wall, yanking it with such force that she pulled the nail out with it, and the two of us stowed our treasures in my Jeep.

When I walked back to the house, Carl, wearing a bemused look, said, "The realtor should have held a garage sale. You're not the only neighbor who was here tonight."

"Who was it?" I asked. "An older woman? A man? A cop?"

I'm afraid I sounded rather breathless and a little kooky, because Carl hesitated to answer me at first. He silently watched his co-worker roll up a frayed area rug from the living room and take it out of the house before answering me.

"It was a man," he said.

"A cop?"

"Don't think so."

"Was his name Nick Foley?"

"He didn't say."

"Kind of muscular looking, with brown hair?"

"Nope. Kind of a chubby, weaselly guy with no sideburns."

"Conner Welch? Our town manager?"

"Dunno. I don't live in Smithwell." Carl shot Emily a sideways glance. "Was I wrong to let him in?"

I moved swiftly, closing the space between me and Carl in a few strides. "Did he take anything?"

"He took a photo frame, like you. He looked around a lot, though, and he seemed to know Sheila Abbottson."

"They're sister and brother," I said. "Where was he looking?"

"Everywhere. He looked like he was assessing the place. Like money-wise." Carl fixed his eyes on me. "Listen, this is more trouble than we're getting paid for."

The poor man looked completely baffled. I took a large backward step. "Never mind, I'm sorry. I know you're only doing your job. I'm upset because the man who lived here was more than a neighbor. He was a friend."

"Ah, I see."

"And we were surprised to see all this—"

"Going on at his house."

"At night," I added.

"We needed to clear everything out before the cleaners got here. But I get it, I get it." He jabbed a thumb in the direction of the stairs. "You ought to talk to the realtor lady. And if you want anything else from the house, just take it. As I say, you're only helping us. But grab it quick."

Carl and his fellow mover hoisted a coffee table waist high and waddled out the door with it.

"This is depressing," Emily said.

"Grab Ray's typewriter for me?" I said, keeping my voice low. "I'm going to talk to Sheila alone. I might get more out of her that way. I'll meet you in the car."

I mounted the stairs for the second floor, and when I came to the landing, I called out for Sheila, a little

120

surprised that she hadn't heard me talking to Carl.

"What do you want *now?*" she called back. "I'm down the hall, and I'm working."

I caught her drift. She *had* heard me downstairs and she wasn't thrilled to see me. I traced her voice to Ray's bedroom, where she was ransacking the top drawer of a nightstand, a sight that irked me no end. Ray was gone, yes, and Ray's son had hired this woman, but she lacked the basics of human consideration.

"What are you looking for?" I asked her, infusing my tone with as much irritation as I'd sensed in hers.

She spun back, her eyebrows arching in indignation. "I'm doing what Owen Landry asked me to do. There's a family heirloom watch we can't find. I don't want the movers to take it."

"Oh."

"Yes, *oh.* And you?"

"I thought I could pick up the Ball jars, but I see they're gone."

Sheila's shoulders drooped a little and her eyebrows relaxed. Perhaps she felt a little guilty, disposing of them so quickly, and I considered how that might play in my favor when I asked her about Alana's murder. Which I was bracing myself to do. Before she could say anything about the jars, I said, "Did you hear that the police are calling Ray's death a homicide?"

"No, I hadn't heard. Are they really?"

"It's not much of a surprise."

"It is to *me.*" Sheila dropped to the bed, looking a little shell-shocked. "There was a *murder* in this house? Now I'll have to tell potential buyers." She lowered her head and began to massage her temples. "This will affect the price. I know it. Anything bad that happens in a house always does. Buyers take advantage of it and wheedle the price down."

Rolling my eyes and biting my tongue, I looked away from her to a chest of drawers next to Ray's bed. On it was another photo, this one of Ray and his wife, Donna. Focusing on that rather than what I really wanted to say to Sheila at that moment, I asked her if I could keep the photo.

"What? Fine," she said with a dismissive wave of her hand.

As I reached for it, Minette poked her head from behind the frame and I gasped involuntarily.

"What now?" Sheila said, shooting daggers at me.

"Nothing."

"You look like you've seen a ghost."

"No, no. I haven't. I've never seen a ghost in my life. Not once. Have you?"

Judging by her expression, she thought I was out of my mind. "Is that photo what you came for?"

"Yes, I think so."

When Sheila returned to her ransacking duties, I held open my jacket pocket and jerked my head toward it, signaling Minette. She dove for it, and I seized the photo frame to cover for her in case Sheila's peripheral vision was top-notch. "Can I ask you a few questions about the Alana Williams murder six years ago?"

She groaned. "Conner told me you were going on about that. Are you a detective now? If I answer your questions, will you leave and not come back?"

"Deal." She didn't like me, I didn't like her, and Ray wouldn't have liked her either, so that made being brusque with her easier. "The police questioned you because you were seen arguing with Alana the night before she died. What were you arguing about?"

Sheila turned on me, her eyes blazing. "She was interfering with a sale, and that was detrimental not only to me, but to Nick Foley. He wanted to sell his nursery—no, he *needed desperately* to sell his nursery—and she talked him out of it."

"How did she do that?"

Sheila laughed. "How do you think? Nick succumbed to her pretty face. Alana almost lost him his livelihood and lost his employees their jobs. And for what? Because she liked visiting the nursery. She liked plants. It was selfish of her, and I told her so."

"But Nick must have turned things around."

"Only just, and Alana had no way of knowing he would. He could've crashed, gone into bankruptcy."

"How many other women were seeing Nick at the time?" I asked. "Were you?"

Sheila erupted with a donkey's bray of laughter. "Are you mental? Me and Nick? I was happily married then, and for your information, there was no attraction. For either of us. Are we finished? I have sixteen hours before my first showing, and now I have to explain a murder in the house."

CHAPTER 16

I thanked Sheila—a difficult thing to do—and went out the back door, photo frame in hand, so I could talk to Minette before seeing Emily. How was I going to carry her in my pocket back to the Jeep? I was afraid I'd sit on her. I walked well away from the house, pulled my pocket wide, but looked straight ahead, out into the woods.

"What were you doing?" I asked, without taking my eyes from the trees. "You could have been caught, and Sheila Abbottson is *not* a nice woman."

"People don't see me," Minette said. "Even when they do, they think they don't."

"How did you get in Ray's house?"

"I can get in anywhere."

"Great, great. Did you want to see his house again? Is that it?"

"Yes. And I heard things to help you."

"You did?" I stared down at my pocket. I couldn't help it. I only hoped no one was watching me because I must have looked—in Sheila's terminology—mental. "Tell me, quickly."

"Sheila the mean realtor lady was talking with her idiot brother."

"Minette, his name is Conner."

124

"That's what Sheila called him. Idiot brother."

"Fair enough. Go on."

"She called the movers the idiot movers."

"Okay. Tell me what you heard that will help me."

"First they talked about money. Her idiot brother said one big sale like Foley's nursery will set her up for years. And Sheila said, 'That idiot Foley is doing too well, even with his big overhead.' She wondered how he does it. Then her idiot brother said Detective Rancourt made him think about Alana again."

"Really?" I swung back to the house, searched the upstairs windows to make certain I wasn't being watched, then did another about-face. "What else?"

"Sheila said, 'Just drop it,' and the idiot brother said he and Rancourt were talking about Alana because Rancourt started it, not him. He said it was because it's almost the anniversary of her death. And then Ray of the Forest came up to them and told Rancourt that he had things wrong and Rancourt looked worried after that."

"Why exactly was he worried?"

"That's what Sheila asked."

"And the idiot brother said?"

"He said, 'I'm not sure. I'm beginning to wonder if I've had it all wrong.' Then a mover shouted upstairs to ask him a question and he went downstairs."

The back door creaked open. I let go of my pocket and wheeled back.

"Kate? I wondered what happened to you." Emily trotted down the back steps and walked out to where I stood, still trying my best to appear enthralled by the woods. "What did Sheila say?"

I told her.

"I can't picture her and Nick either," she said. "You know, you can always see Ray's house and yard again. Just take a walk through the woods back here."

"It won't be his house in a few days."

She wrapped her arms about her, fending off the chill night air. "It doesn't feel like his now. They're cleaning the place out like he never existed. Wiping it clean. What's that photo?"

"Ray and Donna in happier times." I showed her the frame I'd taken from atop the chest of drawers.

"I put his typewriter in the Jeep, and I took a vase from a kitchen cabinet. The one Ray always put his cut peonies in, remember?"

"Good. I'm glad. Ray would want you to have it." I hooked my arm right through hers, mindful that my left pocket held Minette, and set out for my car. "Come on, let's go. I've had enough of this."

We didn't talk on the short drive home. I was thinking about Ray and how his death had changed everything on Birch Street, and I suppose Emily was too. I parked in my garage and she walked home on the flagstone path, taking her now-treasured vase with her. Minette remained sheltered in my pocket until I reached the kitchen, where she flew out and up to the hutch, landing inside a teacup. There was something about my Wedgwood she liked.

"You have to be more careful, Minette," I said. "What if the mean realtor lady had seen you?"

"She wouldn't have believed it, Kate." Minette leaned forward and rested her arms on the rim of the teacup. "She would have said 'No, no, no, it can't be.'"

"Like me?" I smiled, slung my jacket over the back

of a kitchen chair, and sat. "Someone like Sheila Abbottson would go after you with a broom and a can of bug spray, whether or not she thought you were a fairy or even real. People can be dangerous."

"I know this. I know more than you think."

There was that middle-aged know-it-all tone again, emanating from the innocent, porcelain-like features of a child. "How old are you?"

"I was created fifty-seven years ago."

"You're *fifty-seven*? You don't seem that old."

"It's not old."

"Tell my bones that. I'm fifty."

"I know. It was your birthday."

"Minette, you've said things like that before. You know this and that about me, and you've been watching me—why? Why have you been watching me?"

"I followed Ray of the Forest."

"You mean when he visited me?"

"Sometimes."

"What about other times?"

"Sometimes I came without him and watched you in your garden. I'm going to fly now." She hopped out of the teacup and onto the hutch shelf, and in one brisk movement she leapt from the shelf, went horizontal, barreled for the table, and hovered two feet from my face, grinning mischievously.

Endearing though she was, and though my fear of her had almost completely disappeared, I was still unnerved by the idea that she had watched me. "Do you watch Emily MacKenzie?"

"Only when she's here."

"Then why did you watch me in my garden?"

127

Minette floated to the table, sat cross-legged, and gazed up at me, her chin in her hands. "You're kind to ladybugs and crickets."

"Yes, you said that before."

"And even worms."

"You wouldn't know that unless you had reason to watch me *before* you saw me with crickets and worms."

"And I saw you with ladybugs before."

"You're being evasive."

Round-eyed and suddenly slow of language, she said, "What's evasive?"

I lowered my chin and fixed my gaze on her. "We've been talking for more than twenty-four hours and the one word you don't know is *evasive?*"

Minette bit her lower lip and then said, "You don't believe."

"What are you talking about? Believe? I'm talking to a fairy! How much more believing do I have to be?" I asked, punctuating my words with wild hand gestures. "If I didn't believe you existed, I'd check myself into a facility right now. If I didn't believe, would I have taken you out of Ray's house in my pocket, risking looking like a complete lunatic? Or kept you secret from Emily, my best friend? Who, by the way, will probably check me into a facility herself before this is over."

The kitchen was silent in the wake of my tantrum. *Chewing out a tiny, defenseless creature. That's not good, Kate.* I was about to say something kind but ambiguous when I saw a look of pity in Minette's eyes. That was it. I was *not* going to be pitied. "Don't do that," I said.

"I'm not doing anything." Minette sat on her hands, closed her eyes, and held her breath, making herself look

128

small and harmless, I supposed.

"Don't do that either. Start breathing or you'll pass out."

She exhaled and opened her emerald eyes. "You think you're ordinary."

"I *am* ordinary, and I don't mind being ordinary. In fact, I like it." I rose and pushed my chair back. "I just don't want an ordinary *life*."

"What is that?"

"A life that goes on and on in a pointless way," I said. "Everything is hard, nothing is good, nothing means much of anything. That kind of life."

"That's not an ordinary life, that's a bad life."

"Regardless, no one wants a life like that."

"You don't believe."

"Are we back there again? I'm going to bed."

Minette flitted slowly upward, her pink wings beating. "You don't believe in *God*."

"I told you I do."

"You don't believe he sent me to you."

"Don't." I flung my finger at her, and for the first time I felt real anger, though not at Minette. My anger was without aim, coming from a previously unmined depth in my soul, bubbling up and taking me by surprise. "Don't say that. He doesn't send anyone, and he sure doesn't send four-inch flying creatures to fifty-year-old widows in Smithwell, Maine. Don't you *dare*."

Still hovering, Minette squeezed her tiny hands together. "All right, Kate. I won't. I won't." Her voice was plaintive, imploring.

And I felt like a jerk.

"I need to go to bed to think and write before I turn

in," I told her. "There's a lot of information swimming around in my head, and I have to make sense of it." I started for my bedroom, but Minette cut me off at the stairs.

"I must help. I didn't tell you everything the mean realtor lady and her idiot brother said."

"Fine. I'll open my bedroom door in three minutes."

I trudged up the stairs, changed to my pajamas, plumped my pillows so I could sit comfortably in bed, and retrieved a notepad and pen from my nightstand. Then I opened my door. Minette grinned at me as though we hadn't just had words—well, as though *I* hadn't just had words—and flew to the end of my bed. I got in and, pen poised, asked her what more of Sheila and Conner's conversation she had overheard. "Did Conner go back upstairs after talking to the movers?"

"He did. And Sheila asked him what he thought he had all wrong about Alana's murder. And he said he was beginning to think the case could have been solved if people had wanted it solved. Isn't that scary, Kate? Then Sheila said, 'Don't bring it up again. I don't want any part of it.' Then Conner looked afraid. He said, 'This is troubling' and 'Ray should never have opened this can of worms.' Then he didn't say anything more. That's all I heard."

"Good heavens, Minette. Do you know what that means? Conner thinks the police are involved. The police! I wish I'd never talked to Rancourt."

CHAPTER 17

After a restless night, I rose late the next morning. Minette had spent the night in a teacup on the hutch, and she was wide awake and sitting on a kitchen counter when I got up—raring to go, she said, though I'd already told her she couldn't follow me to Foley's Nursery. I made a breakfast of buttered toast and almond tea, and to my surprise Minette ate the bit of toast I offered her. It was the first thing I'd seen her eat since discovering her in my hutch.

"I'm worried about you," I told her. "What are you eating?"

"The forest is full of food," she replied. "Nuts and roots and berries. In the spring there are leeks and wild watercress by the river. Oh, Kate, leeks are delicious! I love spring in the forest."

"What about the fall and winter? How do you survive?"

"Roots, wild radishes, and reindeer moss." Minette flitted to the table, where I was sitting with my cup of tea. "And maple syrup from the trees. It's *superb*."

"Superb, is it? Well, I think it's about time I bought some honest-to-goodness real maple syrup. If I get the chance, I'll pick some up this afternoon."

She grinned and gleefully tossed back her light brown hair. "I don't have to fly to the trees?"

"You don't ever have to again if you don't want to," I said. "And you can stay in my house, out of the cold, for as long as you want." I rose, took my jacket from the chair, where I'd left it the night before, and dug around for my car keys in the pocket. "I have to pick up Emily and head to Foley's Nursery."

"I don't like that nursery," Minette said. "I don't like Nick Foley, I don't like Sheila the realtor, I don't like Conner the idiot brother, I don't like—"

"What about Irene Carrick, the author Ray told about fairies? I bought that orchid in the living room because of her. I thought you'd like it."

"I do like it! I like orchids, but Irene the writer doesn't believe—" Minette pressed her lips together, hard, and peered at me through barely opened eyes.

"Never mind that. Why don't you like the nursery?"

"Ray of the Forest thought it was a place of suspicious activity."

I dropped like a rock to my chair. "What kind of activity? Did he explain?"

"No, he only said suspicious, but I think it was about money."

"Suspicious activities often are."

I'd wondered how Nick Foley went from near bankruptcy to solvency in a short period of time, especially since I hadn't noticed an uptick in his business over the past six years, after he'd supposedly considered selling the nursery and then irked Sheila Abbottson by declining to do so. Was he engaged in something illegal? Was that why his financial fortunes had improved?

With a newfound and healthy concern about what hornet's nest I might poke by asking Nick questions, I headed out to my Jeep, picked up Emily at her house, and drove out to the nursery. As I drove down the Bog Road, under a blanket of gray rain clouds, I told her I was skeptical of the nursery's miracle recovery six years ago, right about the time Alana had been murdered, though I didn't say what—or who—had spurred my skepticism.

"If Nick suddenly came into enough money to save his nursery," Emily said, "then he's involved in something dangerous. Imagine what the overhead is with a place like that. Thousands of dollars a month. The water, the electricity, the employees' pay. So what illegal activity can earn you that kind of money?"

"A large nursery is a handy place to hide all kinds of things," I replied, "from illegal plants to stolen jewelry to drugs. A place to hide things or to transfer things from one person to another."

"What kind of illegal plants?"

"Maybe invasive species. Maine recently made selling a lot of popular trees and shrubs illegal." But immediately I discounted that theory. Bringing in Norway maples and other plants now deemed invasive was too risky, too easily discovered, and as far as I could see, wouldn't bring a substantial reward. No, I leaned toward drugs, stolen jewelry, or some other small, pricey, and illicit commodity.

I pulled into Foley's parking lot, casting my eyes about for Nick. "He must be inside," I said. "Let me talk to him alone, so he doesn't feel like he's being ganged up on. It's possible he's completely innocent of any wrongdoing."

"All right, I'll keep my distance. But I'm keeping an eye on you."

"I'm counting on it."

Just inside the front door, Emily and I separated. Wandering around the tables and winding my way through the hanging flower baskets, I searched for Nick but couldn't find him. Distracted by the fairy gardens display, I headed there for another look at the alpine plants and tiny houses, most of them too small for a real fairy. If all fairies were like Minette, they needed ample room to fly. I wasn't sure that even *my* house was sufficiently large.

I was reaching for a plastic pot of baby's tears when I heard the crunch of pea gravel behind me.

"Fairy gardens, Kate?"

I felt the muscles in my neck tighten. I hesitated and then willed my body to turn, bringing the plastic pot of baby's tears to my chest and clinging to it with both hands.

"Nick. Hi. Why not fairy gardens?" I attempted to smile and felt my mouth twitch. Goodness knows what I looked like.

"I didn't think it was your style. Now, Ray Landry was interested in fairy gardens for some freaky reason, but I think he was reverting to his childhood. You haven't hit that stage yet."

"Maybe I never left that stage."

Nick jammed his hands into his soil-covered jeans. "Maybe we're all still there, huh? Just trying to get by, day by day. Trying to grab hold of something to keep us going, get us out of bed in the morning. It's the way of the world."

"You're getting philosophical, Nick."

"I blame old age," he said. His lips were pinched in a strained smile. "Not Ray's kind of old age, but old enough."

"What's Ray's kind of old age?"

"Dotty. Seeing things. Imagining things."

"What did he imagine?"

He flung his hands in the air, startling me. "That the world is a bright and shining place, full of misery but full of enough wonder to compensate for that. Full of gifts from an invisible and silent god. A place where trees clap their hands and rocks sing, as he used to tell me."

Nick was talking like a man on the edge. What had brought about this change in him? *The guilty flee when no man pursues.*

"Can I ask you something?" I said.

"I must be psychic. I knew you were going to say that."

I was about to burn any friendship bridge I had with Nick. I knew that, and at first I was reluctant to light the match, but Nick's bizarre attitude and his disdain for Ray were making it easier.

"Sheila Abbottson told me you were going to sell your nursery six years ago but you changed your mind. Can I ask why?"

Nick looked as though I'd slapped him. "She told you that? That's confidential by anyone's definition."

"I know, and I'm sorry. Sheila was explaining why she argued with Alana Williams the night she was killed."

"Wow. Man. Wow." Nick scratched his head, his growing indignation overtaking his verbal skills. "Unbelievable. You and Ray."

"Ray? Did he ask you that too? Nick, if you're in trouble, you need to talk to someone."

"What kind of trouble do you think I'm in? You know so much—tell me."

"I don't know, but you seem unusually upset."

He snorted. "Shut up, Kate. Don't psychoanalyze me."

I sucked in my breath. I'd never seen this hard, nasty side of Nick Foley. And I was only getting started. I took firmer hold of the baby's tears. "Did you give Alana Williams a heart-shaped necklace?"

Expecting denial, I was surprised when Nick folded his arms over his chest in a defiant posture and said, "Yeah, I did. What about it? I gave her a necklace. And before that I gave her a crystal bird. I even gave her a few books. Big deal. You don't think the cops know I was seeing her? Get real. The way lips flap in this town, half of Smithwell knew."

"When we talked about her, you pretended that she was just a customer."

He leaned toward me, his voice a whisper. "Because it's not your business. It's not this town's business. We kept things private because tongues wag."

"I know it's not my business, Nick, but I'm trying to find out who killed Ray."

"Alana died six stinking years ago. She's got nothing to do with Ray Landry."

"You saw Alana the morning of the day she died."

"I told you that yesterday. She was here buying a fern."

"Before classes instead of after. Right. Was she wearing the necklace at the time?"

136

"Yes. I gave it to her that morning and put it on her. Satisfied?"

"Did the police ask you about the necklace?"

"No, they're weren't as captivated by it as you seem to be. It's a piece of jewelry." He brushed his hands together, wiping off the dirt and, I was sure, figuratively wiping me out of his life. "If you're done grilling me, I have work to do. Buy something or don't. Whatever you want. But then leave." He stomped off, walking as far from me as the dimensions of the building would allow.

I set down my pot of baby's tears. So on the last morning of her life, Alana had left Foley's Nursery wearing her new necklace. She was then lured into the woods—or followed someone in—she was murdered, and her necklace disappeared. If Nick had killed her and then taken the necklace to hide his relationship with her, why would he subsequently admit that relationship to the police? And why was he now admitting that he'd given Alana the necklace the morning she died? It didn't make sense. Unless . . .

Oh, I didn't like what I was thinking. It made me feel unsafe, without a place to turn.

Emily came striding up to me, her feet slapping the pea gravel, her eyes as big as saucers. "Veins were popping in Nick's neck. I could see them bulging all the way back at the cash registers. What did you say to him?"

"I struck a nerve."

"Did you learn anything?"

"Yes, but I don't know what to do with it."

"I learned something too. One of the employees thinks Nick Foley is up to no good." Wearing a satisfied grin, Emily nodded in a vigorous yup-you-got-it kind of way. "I'll tell you something else. She was working here six years ago, the day Alana bought the fern. Apparently, Alana wanted another plant from a fresh shipment and Nick wouldn't let her have it. He said the new plants were in quarantine, but this employee doesn't know if that was true."

"Out to my car. I don't feel safe here."

"Do you think Nick had—"

"Don't say another word." I grabbed Emily by the arm and towed her out the door and toward my car.

We strapped our seatbelts on and I started the engine, not intending to let the Jeep warm up.

"Slow down, it's Marie St. Peter," Emily said, jerking her chin at the windshield. "I recognize her from the police website."

"Where?" By the time I saw Sergeant St. Peter, she was heading inside the nursery. "What do you think she's doing here?"

"Maybe the police want to question Nick again. It could be they're not as blind as we think they are."

I backed out of my parking spot, my mind reeling. "It's not their blindness I'm worried about, Emily."

CHAPTER 18

Emily and I returned to my house for tea, lunch, and a good talk about what we had learned at Foley's—and what we were going to do with that information. Again I made a ruckus when I entered, knocking the mud from my already-clean shoes as I stood outside the door, letting the door creak as I opened it—alerting Minette to our arrival, though she'd probably heard me coming up the driveway. I wanted so much to tell Emily that one of Ray's mythical creatures was in my house at that very moment. But I didn't need her thinking I'd gone around the bend. She already thought I was, well, different.

Emily hooked her purse and jacket on the back of a kitchen chair and sat. "First things first. Make me some tea and tell me who your suspects are now. I want to know if you've whittled down the list."

As I filled the kettle with water, I thought about Emily's question. Why was Irene Carrick still on my suspect list? Really, what had she done or said? I didn't like her thinking that Ray had been suffering from dementia, but from her perspective, that was a reasonable conclusion.

"If we agree that the person who killed Ray also killed Alana—" I began.

"We do."

"—then not Irene Carrick," I said, setting the kettle on the stove.

"You said that before."

"I'm confirming it. She was too old six years ago and she's too old now. Besides, she loved Ray in her own way. I think she's heartbroken he's gone. She said he was healthy enough to live another ten years, and I agree. Plus, she had no motive to kill Alana. She even volunteered information to the police so her friend Norma wouldn't have to speak to them."

"Okay, agreed. Check."

I took a Wedgwood teapot and two matching cups from the hutch. Irene, the old Mainer, would have deemed them extravagant. "And I'm ruling out Sheila Abbottson. You should have heard her when I asked if she'd had an affair with Nick. She genuinely thought I was off my rocker. Six years ago all she was thinking about was the money she'd get from selling the nursery, and the only reason she got angry with Alana was because she *believed* Alana talked Nick out of the sale."

"Sheila might have killed Alana for that. With Alana out of the way, Nick maybe decides to sell."

"Do you really think Alana was the reason Nick decided not to sell his nursery? It's what Sheila thought, but I don't see it. If Nick was near bankruptcy, he needed a better reason than Alana's love of plants to hold on to a money pit."

"'Your loving don't pay my bills,' as the song goes."

I sat down, waiting for the kettle to boil, wishing I could fill some of the giant information holes in our mystery tapestry. There was so much we either didn't know or were only guessing at. "Is there a way to find out what kind of money Nick's nursery was pulling in six years ago? Can you drop Laurence's name?"

"If his nursery business sells stock—"

"Which it doesn't."

She held up a finger. "If Nick started bankruptcy proceedings—"

"Which he may have."

"Laurence has a friend or two at the Town Office. Our information could be sitting in a file there, waiting to be discovered."

"What exactly does your husband do for a living? I mean, when he's not in Afghanistan or Hungary. Remind me."

"You know, hotels, construction. He makes friends in far-flung places," she said with a wry smile. "It's what he did before hotels that I wonder about. I know the official line—he traveled to American embassies around the world—but what he actually did is beyond my pay grade and I don't ask him too many questions about it. All I know is I can drop his name and doors open, even in little Smithwell. I'll bet Detective Rancourt knows him."

"I wouldn't be surprised. Is there someone you can call now?"

"Give me five minutes."

While Emily made the call from the living room, I put leftover pizza in the oven to reheat, poured hot water into my teapot, and took the pot to the table to let the leaves steep. What did someone who traveled to embassies around the world do? I wondered, fingering the teapot Michael had purchased for me in Portland.

"Government work" had been Emily's standard reply when anyone asked, but that could mean anything from filling out paperwork to contacting other countries' ambassadors to being a spy. Whatever the case, Laurence's name opened a myriad of doors.

Two minutes later Emily returned, looking like the cat that ate half a dozen canaries.

"According to Frank Pelletier—"

"A friend of Laurence's?"

"Naturally. He says Nick Foley started bankruptcy proceedings but pulled out six years and one month ago."

"One month before Alana was killed."

"Precisely. Nick was in a terrible bind. He filed because he was days away from catastrophe, as Frank put it. When he found out Nick stopped proceedings, he assumed he'd been able to secure a private loan. He said the bank wouldn't have loaned him a cent, though. They would've advised him to sell—and at a reduced price so he could make a quick sale and pay them back."

"So Sheila was telling the truth about Nick's situation. Hold that sieve over our cups," I said as I poured the tea.

"Nick's father started that nursery," Emily went on. "Did you know that?"

"It's a family inheritance. Giving it up would be devastating."

"But there's no way Nick got a private loan." Emily blew across her tea and then sipped it.

"I agree. That would be throwing good money after bad, and that means the money that saved the nursery was not legit. Do you think the police looked into that?"

"If they did, it didn't lead them anywhere. Barney

Fifes."

"I trust Ray's instincts on this. He thought there were suspicious activities going on in that nursery."

Emily raised an eyebrow. "Did he? When did he say that?"

I wanted to smack my own forehead. What could I say? Ray told a fairy and a fairy told me? "He didn't say it. I saw it. He wrote it down." How I *hated* lying to her. "It was in that pamphlet somewhere."

"But nothing specific?"

"No."

"Wow. Ray was on top of things."

"Much more than most people think."

"But Kate, that's what got him killed."

The stove timer sounded and I rose to take the pizza out of the oven. "Whatever Nick is up to at his nursery, he's not doing it alone. He's in cahoots with at least one other person."

"Cahoots, agreed. Check."

"We still don't know if he killed Alana," I said, bringing the pizza to the table. "Why would he kill her and then steal back the necklace? He must have known that would look bad for him. He gave it to her at the nursery, put it on her, and she walked out of the nursery wearing it. How many employees saw it on her? How many people at Smithwell Middle School saw it on her that morning?"

"Why would Nick kill her at all?" Emily asked, grabbing a slice. "Why would anyone? She was a harmless schoolteacher."

"She was a threat to someone, and my money is on Nick. That whole plant-quarantine thing? He was hiding something. Literally."

"You mean hiding something in the new plant shipment. So you're also crossing Conner Welch off your list?"

"He didn't have a motive." And judging by what Minette had told me about his exchange with Sheila in Ray's house, he was as bewildered by Alana's murder as I was. He hadn't talked like a guilty man, he'd talked like a confused and somewhat frightened one. "What do you think about Rancourt and St. Peter? Are they still on our list?"

As Emily chewed, she pondered my question, and as she pondered, I could see that she had never fully considered that someone on the police force might have killed Alana, or that the police might have been involved in a cover-up after her death. It shook her as it shook me. "If the police are a part of this, we're in serious trouble."

"With nowhere to turn," I said. Suddenly starving, I dug into my pizza.

"We're back to *why*," Emily said. "Why kill a schoolteacher? Let's say she found out what Nick was up to."

"Mmm," I mumbled with a nod of agreement.

"And she threatened to go to the police. Would he kill her for that? Is he that kind of man?"

"Is he the kind of man to get involved in something illegal in order to save his nursery?" I asked rhetorically. "If our theory is right, Nick *did* get involved in something illegal, and maybe something very serious. He thought he could get away with it for however long it took to clear his debts, but Alana found out. A young schoolteacher at her first job, starting fresh in life—she would have been

144

appalled by the whole seedy matter. Even if she didn't threaten to go to the police, she would've made it clear that she didn't approve. Nick couldn't take a chance that she'd turn on him. It's not hard to imagine him killing her to avoid prison time."

"So why give her a necklace on the day he killed her?"

"Could be it was a last-ditch attempt to win her over. He was saying, 'Look what I can buy for you now. And there's more where that came from.'" I shrugged. "Just a guess."

"We need answers." Emily slapped her knees and stood. "And I need to go home to wait for the electrician. He's coming to take a look at my dodgy dining-room can lights. Thankfully, they're the least useful lights in the house. In the meantime, I'm going to make more calls to Frank Pelletier. I think he enjoys the intrigue."

Emily bent and gave me a hug before setting out for her house. The second the front door shut, Minette flew out of the hutch and landed on the table. She'd been there all along, sitting inside a creamware jug on the top shelf.

"What if Emily had heard you?" I said.

"No one hears me if I'm quiet. If they do, they think I'm an insect."

"And then they come after you with a flyswatter."

I rose and began to clear the table. Minette was both wise and utterly naive. How had Ray kept her safe?

"I'm thinking something," she said.

"What's that?" I answered without turning around. I set the plates and cups in the sink.

"I'm thinking that Nick of the nursery was hiding things, and that he killed Alana."

"Yeah." I leaned back on the sink, rubbing my weary eyes. "Maybe he was hiding things in fresh shipments of plants. The ones he supposedly quarantines."

Minette flapped her wings and shot for my face, stopping inches from my nose and hovering like a hummingbird. "But he does quarantine plants sometimes. I know he does."

"Did Ray ever take you to Foley's?"

"Twice. In his pocket. I love the smell there. But Kate, plants are too small. The pots are filled with soil, and if they're not, the plants die."

"Did you see Nick when you went to the nursery?"

"Yes. Do you know what else I saw? Nick taping big bags that had long tears in them."

"Compost bags?" I recalled my visit to the nursery yesterday, when I'd seen Nick taping compost bags. I'd assumed the bags had been torn in transit.

"Compost and soil and bark. Both times, Kate. I'm thinking Nick has too many tears in the bags."

CHAPTER 19

"Someone is hiding something in the bags," I said. "Minette, you're right! All those big, ripped bags! I'd fire a supplier who shipped so many bags in that condition."

Minette did a mid-air, 360-degree loop and landed on her feet atop the microwave on my counter. "I knew! I knew! He's hiding things in the bags!"

"It's a perfect place to hide . . . something . . . I don't know what. What is he sneaking in or out of the nursery?" I let go with a little roar of frustration.

"You have to find the bags before Nick touches them. Does Nick tear them open or does someone else do the tearing open before Nick sees them?"

"I don't know, but Nick has to be working with someone else. He's allowing his compost bags to be used as mules."

"Mules?"

"Never mind, it's an expression."

"But we don't know—" Minette stopped and put a finger to her lips. "There's someone driving to your house. I hear a big car."

I strode quickly to the side door and pulled back the curtain over the window just enough to get a look outside as a black Smithwell Police SUV lumbered up the drive.

"Hide, Minette," I said, letting the curtain fall.

"Is it a bad person?" she asked.

"I don't know." For a moment I felt frozen in place. I didn't trust Rancourt and didn't want him in my house. If he trapped me inside, I'd have no way out. "I'm going out the front door so I can talk to him outside," I told Minette. "You stay hidden in case I have to come inside for some reason. I mean it—stay hidden."

I grabbed a broom from the closet in the foyer, rushed outside, and began to sweep leaves from the bench by the door. Anything to look like I had a reason to be outside my house.

"It's a never-ending job this time of year," I heard Rancourt say.

Wheeling back, I saw him walking toward me, smiling affably. The gruff man I'd met at the police station had vanished for the moment.

"Yes, but autumn leaves are nice." I had no idea what that meant or why I'd said it, except that I needed to say something and say it fast.

He stopped a few feet from me, stuffed his hands in his raincoat pockets, and looked out over my front lawn. "Until you have to rake them. I hope you don't take care of this yard yourself."

"I pay someone to do the big jobs."

"Good, good."

Leaning my broom against the side of the house, I said, "How do you know I don't have a husband to do it for me?"

His hands still in his pockets, he looked back at me. "You're not a fool, Mrs. Brewer. You must know I checked your background. You came to visit me—that's unusual for a start—and I'm investigating the murder of your neighbor." He shot me a semi-apologetic smile. His skin was pasty and his face bloated—fleshy from a diet rich in salt, I thought. "Look, I need to ask you about Mr. Landry. Can we go inside?"

I hesitated just long enough for him to get the idea that I wasn't exactly at ease with him being there.

"That's fine. Can we at least sit down out here?"

"On my landscape boulders out there," I said, pointing.

Undoubtedly thinking I was a bit of a paranoid nut, Rancourt nevertheless followed me and sat on one of the boulders while I sat on another. "Last time I talked to Ray, he sat where you're sitting," I said.

He nodded. "And that was?"

"Day before yesterday. The afternoon of the day he was murdered."

"Look, Mrs. Brewer, I can't tell you much about the investigation—actually, I can't tell you anything more than I already have—but you might be able to help me."

"Officer Bouchard interviewed me the night Ray was found."

Finally Rancourt took his hands out of his pockets. "That was before we had a homicide case. I understand you've been asking questions around town."

"Am I not allowed to do that?"

"You can do as you wish. I can't stop you from talking to people, though I'd prefer it if you were more circumspect. But I think you might be able to help me. Specifically, can you tell me what Mr. Landry said to you when he sat here on this rock?"

I hesitated again and he cocked his head,

bewildered, I thought, that I was waffling over whether to help him.

"Ray told me not to trust anyone I didn't know," I said flatly. "Because of the Alana Williams murder. You may think that's crazy, but as you now know, I live alone. And as you just said, I'm not a fool."

"No," he said with a firm shake of his head. "I don't think you're paranoid. Your neighbor was murdered, and I understand he was writing about Alana Williams at the time. Probably asking people about her. An unsolved murder. That's why he spoke to me in the supermarket the day he died. You're wise to be cautious. More cautious than you're being, in fact."

"You're a policeman," I said.

Rancourt frowned. "Did Mr. Landry tell you to be careful around the police?"

"Not specifically. Just people I don't know, even if they say I'm supposed to trust them."

Rancourt looked away toward the road, his eyes wandering over the scene as though my words had struck an unpleasant chord with him. "But you know something that might help solve his murder? Or *think* you know something?"

His haggard face and the sincere tone in his voice was beginning to win me over, just a little. Well, those things and the fact that I needed to trust someone with the information Ray had given me. "Tell me something first. Why did you disagree with Ray about the Alana Williams crime scene? He's the one who found her, and his memory was sharp."

"He was eighty-one."

"I'm so tired of hearing that."

"It has to be considered."

"No, it doesn't. And frankly, you wouldn't be here if you thought Ray's memory was so fuzzy."

Rancourt laughed. "Points to you."

"So why did you argue with him about the murder scene? It bothered him."

"I'm sorry it did. I couldn't publicly agree that he was right and I was wrong."

I was aghast. "Why? Is your ego that important?"

"I was talking to the town manager. Mrs. Brewer, and the Williams crime scene is on record. Not public record, but still the record. Because it's an unsolved case, we keep things from the public. Do you understand what I'm telling you?"

Rancourt wanted me to read between the lines. "I think I do. Wait here a second." I went inside and retrieved Ray's memoirs and drawing. Before going back out, I reminded Minette that she had to stay hidden. She was itching to follow me outside.

Back on my front lawn, praying I wasn't making a terrible error in judgment, I handed Rancourt the drawing and sat. "Ray drew this after he talked to you in Hannaford's. It's how your recollection of the murder scene differed from his. The two differences are the position of the jacket and the absence of a heart-shaped necklace."

His eyes on the sketch, Rancourt took a deep breath and then exhaled with a small groan.

"There's more," I said. "In his memoirs, he writes about the scene, and the differences are as he notes in that drawing."

At last the detective looked up. "Yes, he mentioned

in the supermarket that his memory of events was clear because he was putting them down in his memoirs. Writing his life story for the first time."

"Welch heard that."

"Welch talks a lot."

I gave Rancourt the precious original copy of Ray's memoirs. "I have copies, but I want this manuscript back."

Rancourt took it in his hands, treating it gently, as though it was a rare piece of work.

"Nick Foley gave Alana that necklace Ray saw," I said. "He put it on her, in the nursery, and she walked out wearing it."

"Mmm."

"I wonder if Alana was having an affair with anyone else."

"Doubt it."

"And there's something else, Detective. Nick Foley was in danger of losing his nursery six years ago. He had terrible financial problems. Sheila Abbottson wanted him to sell the nursery, but according to her, Alana talked him out of it. She loved the nursery. Soon after that, Nick's money troubles pretty much went away. He seems to be doing very well now."

Rancourt shrugged. Now that I'd told him what he'd wanted to know, he was unwilling to return the favor.

"Funny thing about Nick's shipments of compost, soil, and bark," I continued. "So many of the bags are torn."

"Are they?"

"Big bags. Split open. Like Nick took something out of them before stocking the shelves. Or someone else does. He uses an awful lot of tape to correct the problem."

Rancourt was studying me with an intensity that unnerved me. "That's interesting."

"Very. Turns out Ray wasn't so muddled, was he, Detective?"

"Hmm? No. No, he wasn't. But his son told me he was imagining things. He was worried about him."

"Ray Landry had an imagination, and he believed in a lot of good things other people didn't, but he never imagined things that weren't there. He saw what was *there*, he saw it clearly, and he remembered *every single detail*."

"Yes, I think so too, Mrs. Brewer."

Rancourt rose and I flinched.

"I'm sorry," he said, thrusting out a hand. "Mrs. Brewer—Kate—I'm not your enemy."

I got to my feet and took several steps back.

"I've been trying to solve the Alana Williams murder for six years," he said, "and I've been stumped. And blind as a bat."

"Ray saw things," I said softly. *Every single detail.* That's what Ray had told me. He'd said he had remembered every single detail of the murder scene. Nothing had escaped his notice. "He remembered Alana's jacket. When he saw it, it was too neat, just like the killer had left it. The killer who loved her in his own selfish way and felt some remorse after killing her. When you saw it, it was in disarray, as though Alana's pockets had been searched. Maybe so a clue wouldn't be left behind? And then there was the necklace."

Rancourt stared into my eyes, and I saw the pain in his. "I never saw a necklace."

153

"But it was there when Ray found Alana. And that's what he told St. Peter when she interviewed him in her squad car. Just Ray and St. Peter, alone in her car. She never told you Ray saw a necklace, did she? It never entered the official report."

"No."

"That's why you shooed me out of your office when I wanted to talk to St. Peter. You didn't want her to know Ray had told me about the necklace."

"Yes."

"There was no way for you to know she lied."

"It's my job to know."

"I figured Nick had an accomplice. You began to suspect St. Peter after you talked to Ray in the supermarket."

"I'd never heard from Ray's own mouth what he'd seen that day," Rancourt replied, his expression remorseful. "And I moved too slowly after I spoke to him. I should have kept him safe. Stay in your house, Mrs. Brewer, and lock the doors." He whipped around, his stocky frame moving with extraordinary agility, and darted for his SUV. "And call your friend and tell her to do the same!" he shouted.

CHAPTER 20

I did as Rancourt told me—locked and bolted the front door—and from the foyer I went to the kitchen to give Emily a quick call before locking my side and back doors. I reached into my purse and dug around for my phone.

"Mrs. Brewer."

I froze. *Oh, Lord, no*. "I left the back door unlocked," I said, turning slowly around. "Didn't I, Sergeant St. Peter?"

"Seems like it." A sick, twisted grin settled on her face.

"Where's your squad car?"

"Behind your house on Elm Street," she said, gesturing over her shoulder. "Then I just walked through the woods."

"Rancourt just left. He knows what you did."

"What he thinks he knows and what he can prove are two different things."

I shot a glance at my hutch.

"What are you looking at?" St. Peter demanded. She rested her hand on the handle of her gun and simultaneously unsnapped the holster with her thumb. "Do you have a weapon up there?"

"I have *teacups* up there. I don't know about you,

but I don't keep guns in my hutch. What are you doing in my house?"

"You got too nosy," she answered. "Too close. After six years of peace and quiet—why couldn't you keep out of things?"

"Why did you murder my friend?"

She laughed. Actually laughed.

"Me? I'm the cleaner, Mrs. Brewer, not the killer."

"You searched Ray's house for his memoirs."

"Yeah. But after *Foley* killed him. I didn't have anything to do with that."

"So Nick Foley is the killer and you're the cleaner. Detective Rancourt knows that. And he knows you falsified Ray's statement about the Alana Williams murder scene."

"There's no proof of that. Especially with you out of the way. You were the last one to talk to Landry."

"Rancourt has Ray's memoirs. Ray wrote everything down."

"An old man's notes? How long would it take a lawyer to tear into them?"

With a speck of relief I noted that St. Peter's hand was still resting on her gun. She hadn't yet taken the weapon from her holster. I had to stall her. Get her talking. Even argue with her. "How did you do it? You altered the scene, and with Rancourt there."

She grinned again, pleased that I'd asked. It was an opportunity to tell me how brilliant she'd been. "Rancourt trusted me. That's his basic flaw. He trusts his officers. Before he even looked at that woman's body—"

"Alana. Her name was Alana."

"He made a call to the station or the coroner—I

forget which. Doesn't matter. He hung back by his SUV. I had my gloves on, so if he saw me, it looked like I was examining her body. I reached down, ripped off the necklace. Did it in one second. The chain was so light and thin, it didn't even leave a mark on her neck. I looked back at Rancourt and he was still talking. So I searched the woman's jacket pockets. Rancourt didn't suspect a thing."

"You were searching her jacket for anything that might incriminate Nick."

"You got it. And it was insanely easy."

"Did you kill her?"

"Don't be absurd. I was cleaning up Nick's mess. By now you must know that Foley is not the sharpest knife in the drawer. He's useful, but not bright. He didn't have to kill that woman, but he did. He walked her back into the woods—I guess she thought they were going to kiss and hug. He told me she didn't hesitate to follow him. He used a knife he'd stolen years ago. No one could trace it. So he wasn't totally stupid."

"I saw you at the nursery earlier today."

"I needed to hold Nick's hand. Again. He was about to lose it."

"Alana threatened to expose what you two were doing with the nursery."

"My, my, you *have* been a busy and nosy woman."

Fear was making my mouth go dry. "Was it drugs?"

"Old-fashioned cocaine. It's still popular for some weird reason."

"You and Nick are still transporting it, even now."

"Transporting." St. Peter chucked. "I guess you could say that. Do you know what I make as a police sergeant? My paltry salary?"

I thought it odd, but she seemed to want to justify her actions to me. I encouraged her. "Not much, probably. Though more than a first-year schoolteacher, I'll bet. Maybe more than an emergency room nurse or a fireman. You couldn't take on a second job?"

She leaned forward, hissing at me. "After I've worked the sixty I do with the force?"

"That means you make overtime. What is that, time and a half?"

I thought she was going to hit me.

"So you chose a life of drugs and murder because you don't make enough money?" I said. "Was it worth the risk?"

The doorbell rang and I almost jumped out of my skin.

"Don't move," St. Peter warned.

"It must be a neighbor. Whoever it is will think it's strange if I don't answer my door."

"You're not at home. You went out. People do that from time to time."

The doorbell rang again. "Kate?" I heard Emily call. "Where are you? Are you okay?"

"Is that your pesky next-door neighbor?" St. Peter asked.

"Emily. My friend."

St. Peter took a step forward. "Open your door."
"No."

Her hand moved on her gun. "Open your door, let her in. Now."

"What, so you can kill us both? You're going to kill me anyway. You expect me to invite my friend in?"

158

"Kate?" Emily shouted. She knew I was at home. I wouldn't have left without telling her. Her electrician had come and gone, and she'd made her second phone call to Frank Pelletier. She had new information to pass along.

"Open the door now," St. Peter threatened. "All I want to do is convince you to shut up. Both of you. Then I'll leave, and we'll all get on with our lives."

She thought I was an idiot. That was the only explanation. To keep her off balance, I changed tack. "Why did you kill Ray? That sweet, kind man."

"I keep telling you, I'm the cleaner. Foley's the muscle. He shouldn't have killed him, but what's done is done. He said the old guy called 911 but he ripped the phone out of his hands. Then he knew he had to act fast, so he stood behind old Ray and pressed a plastic bag into his face. And why do you think Nick did that—I mean, honestly?" She threw back her head. "This was quiet, dead and over, until that fool started writing about it. He caused his own death. It's his fault."

Emily banged on the door. "Kate, what's wrong? You're scaring me."

"Everything was fine," St. Peter said. "Everything was peaceful, we were all going about our own business in a merry fashion until that crazy old man—"

"If he was crazy—if everyone thought he was crazy—what were you worried about?"

St. Peter was silent for a moment, glaring at me, gnawing at her lower lip. "Rancourt," she said at last. "He never let Williams go. He's one of *those* cops. Has to tie up every loose end. Every year about this time he'd go through the case files again."

"Only he never saw Ray's true statement."

The door banging stopped.

The inside of my mouth was like cotton, my lips were sticking to my teeth, and my legs were so wobbly they trembled. I didn't know how much longer I could stand there, waiting for St. Peter to make her move. What would I do if her gun came out of her holster?

"So Rancourt's one of the good cops," I said.

"He makes twenty thousand more a year than I do."

"You're sick. Murder for money. Two innocent people dead because you wanted money." My hands went to my mouth. I thought I would choke.

St. Peter slipped the gun from her holster. "You think you're so—"

That's all that came out of her mouth, because an instant later Minette charged for the sergeant's face.

St. Peter screamed like a banshee, tumbled backward, and discharged her gun, the round hitting the ceiling. A second later Detective Rancourt burst through the back door and tackled her to the floor.

Feeling faint, I dropped to a kitchen chair, but not before using my last ounce of strength to wave Minette from the kitchen.

"Mrs. Brewer?" Rancourt said.

"I'm fine, I'm fine," I told Rancourt as he handcuffed St. Peter.

"Kate? I heard a gun."

I looked up. A distraught yet relieved Emily was at my back door.

"Stay outside for a minute," I told her, trying to catch my breath.

I heard sirens out on Birch Street, and soon after, Officer Bouchard and another officer whose name I didn't know were escorting Sergeant St. Peter out my front door. Poor out-of-shape Detective Rancourt grimaced his way out of my kitchen, massaging an arm and a rib or two. "I'll be back in a minute," he said.

Emily came in from the back door, staring in wonder at the bullet hole in my ceiling. "Holy cow. Oh, Kate."

"How did Rancourt get here?" I asked her.

"I called the police a minute ago," she began.

"He got here that fast?"

"No, the station told me he was on the way. He'd already called for backup. When I walked around to your back door, he was there, creeping up the steps, trying to be quiet."

"Not quiet enough," I said.

"St. Peter heard him?"

"No," I said, shaking my head and smiling. "The timing couldn't have been better."

"I'll say. Rancourt gave me a look that said *Get out of here, lady*, so I did. Two seconds later, boom! He was busting down your door."

"Oh, Emily, I'm shaking." I lowered my head in my hands.

"Tea," she said firmly. "I'm making herbal tea, nice and hot. You stay right there. Take deep breaths."

I heard knocking on my open front door, and Rancourt asking if he could come in. We were past the point of formality and graciousness, but I appreciated his courtesy.

"Come in, Detective. Please. How did you get here so fast?"

"After I left your house, I called the station to see

where St. Peter was. They couldn't raise her on the radio, so I drove around to Elm Street and saw her squad car parked. She wasn't in it." He sat across from me at the table, studying me for a moment before he asked, "How are you?"

"I'll be all right. I'm just a little wobbly. Thank you."

"I'm sorry you had to go through this."

"St. Peter said Nick killed Alana and Ray, and she was involved with transporting cocaine using the nursery."

"Yup. Nick is being arrested as we speak."

"You must be relieved."

A faint smile crossed his lips. "I'm glad to put this to rest. I'm only sorry I couldn't help Ray Landry."

"You've helped Alana's parents. They no longer have to wonder who killed their daughter."

"St. Peter is spilling it all," Rancourt said. "She's talking like a drunken parrot. In fact, she's ranting about being attacked by a giant pink bee with a human face. She said she was taking her gun from her holster when this dinosaur-sized insect came out of nowhere and flew right for her face. She's shaking like leaf."

"Really?" I said. "How odd. I almost feel sorry for her. It sounds like she's losing her grip on reality."

"A giant pink bee?" Emily said. "What's wrong with the woman? Of course, murderers are unstable to begin with, aren't they?"

"Yup, yup." Rancourt groaned his way to his feet.

"You should go to the hospital," I said.

Emily chimed in, saying, "You look awful, Detective."

"Thank you, ladies. I think. Mrs. Brewer, would you mind coming to the station tomorrow for a statement? Of if you'd rather, I could come here. I know the Pumpkin Festival is tomorrow, so . . ."

"Yes, I have a giant pumpkin to carve." I shot Emily a grin. "But I'll come downtown. It's not a problem."

I glanced at the hutch and then into the living room, but Minette had vanished for the moment—probably up the flue. She was one resourceful little creature. And she, along with Detective Rancourt, had saved my life.

"If you're sure," Rancourt said.

"I'll be there about ten o'clock," I replied. And right after that, I thought, I'll do a little shopping. Pick up a few things. I knew a lovely little store downtown that sold real maple syrup from southern Maine. I'd buy a jug of the stuff. It was the least I could do.

FROM THE AUTHOR

If you enjoyed *Dying to Remember*, would you consider leaving a review on Amazon? Nothing fancy, just a sentence or two. Your help is appreciated more than I can say. Reviews make a *huge* difference in helping readers find the Smithwell Fairies Cozy Mystery Series and in allowing me to continue to write the series. I couldn't do it without your help. Thank you so much!

KARIN'S MAILING LIST

For giveaways, exclusive content, and the latest news on the Juniper Grove Mystery Series and future Karin Kaufman books, sign up to the mail and newsletter list at KarinKaufman.com.

MORE BOOKS BY KARIN KAUFMAN

JUNIPER GROVE COZY MYSTERY SERIES

Death of a Dead Man
Death of a Scavenger
At Death's Door
Death of a Santa
Scared to Death
Cheating Death
Death Trap
Death Knell
Garden of Death
Death of a Professor

ANNA DENNING MYSTERY SERIES

The Witch Tree
Sparrow House
The Sacrifice
The Club
Bitter Roots

CHILDREN'S BOOKS
(FOR CHILDREN AND ADULTS)

The Adventures of Geraldine Woolkins

Made in the USA
Middletown, DE
12 August 2020